HENRIETTA'S JOURNAL

SIMON PLASTER

VOLUME 1

HENRIETTA'S JOURNAL

SIMON PLASTER

2026

All rights reserved. Published by Mossik Press.

mossikpress@mail.com

Library of Congress Cataloguing-in-Publication Data

Plaster, Simon [4.28.2026]

Henrietta's Journal Vol. 1
by Simon Plaster

p. cm
ISBN 979-8-9992429-4-5

1. Humor—Fiction.
2. Oklahoma, United States—Fiction.
3. Law—Fiction.
4. Justice—Fiction.
I. Title

10 9 8 7 6 5 4 3 2 1

Manufactured in the United States of America
First Edition

MAKE CRIME PAY.
BECOME A LAWYER.

Will Rogers

PSYCHOPOMP & CIRCUMSTANCE

IF I COULD TELL YOU
Time will tell nothing but I told you so,
Time only knows the price we have to pay;
If I could tell you I would let you know.

W.H. Auden

SIMON PLASTER

CHAPTER 1

YOU'VEBEEN WARNED! *We grind to feed the faces and souls of the heatseekers who dare to dance with the devil.*

Henrietta exited the Chicken & Wolf cafe—a fast food joint across a street from the University of Tulsa campus—and headed back to class. She had recently read that spicy foods such as the HOT AS HELL nuggets listed on the eatery's menu board were good for sparking brain function and—now almost finished with a two-day course at a nearby Acheron Academy—felt a need to boost her attention, motivation and memory, not to mention stay awake.

Except for a fella named Oscar North, who admitted to already flunking the Oklahoma bar exam five times, most others cramming for an upcoming exam were likely about twenty-five years in age after three years of law school more or less immediately following graduation from college. She her own self, now past thirty, had not got through correspondence college in a timely manner while holding down jobs, and had took five years to finish studying at the online Judge Judy Sheindlin School of Law.

So lectures by experts on subjects such as Civil Procedure, Contracts, Criminal Law, Real Property, and Torts—wrongful acts leading to civil legal liability—had only served to semi-remind her of things she had forgot, or never got a grip on.

At the side of a Harvard Avenue antiques store called Down Memory Lane, a flight of concrete stairs led to the underground academy. Over the steel door at the basement entrance a painted sign said:

ABANDON ALL HOPE, YE WHO ENTER HERE
Under a low ceiling lined with pipes and strips of fluorescent lights, most of the other crammers were already re-seated at right-handed desks that looked to have been salvaged from an oldtime high school.

Oscar North had brought a sack lunch to class and chose to have it by hisself, but now... Dang it, back-row desks on both sides of him were re-occupied.

Returned to her prior front-row desk next to a not so appealing fella named R. Marcus Burnham, redheaded but—wearing coat, tie, thick glasses, and having a grating nasal sort of voice—a lot like the annoying blue-haired lawyer on the *Simpsons* tv show.

As overhead pipes gurgled and lights flickered, onto a low platform stepped an old man...near to seventy by the look of him...heavyset and jowly, with deadish bloodshot eyes...wearing a gray robe and one of those flat-topped graduation caps with an also black tassel hanging from it. No doubt the instructor listed on the cram course program for its final session: Dean of the Acheron Academy, Virgil Griswold.

Onto a wall-mounted blackboard, the Dean—left-handed like her own self—chalked in pink:
VESTIBULE of HELL
"Given the low bar for admission, most of you will probably pass this month's exam and become members of the American legal fraternity presently consisting of approximately 1.3 million others," he then said. "To forewarn you of the consequences of your passage, I shall—in this final hour—endeavor to act as a kind of psychopomp, which means..."

"In ancient Greek mythology, a psychopomp is a deity, sometimes appearing as a cuckoo bird," said the redheaded smarty-pants beside her, "with responsibility to non-judgmentally guide souls of the deceased into afterlife. In Jungian psychology, the term means mediator between the unconscious and conscious realms."

Ohhh... others in attendance ohhhed.

"Indeed, that shall be my approximate endeavor: not to 'guide your passage into' but to provide you with a glimpse into a place of woe and eternal pain among those who are morally neutral: the opportunists who take either side as theirs, neither in Hell nor out of it, constantly stung by guilty conscience and remorse."

Ohhh…

"Unless you turn back from 'crossing the bar' into Purgatory, during a period of, say, ten years—if you stick to your ill-chosen profession—approximately one out of three of you will be addicted to alcohol and/or other mind-numbing substances. In roughly the same proportion, you will be divorced, you will have at least contemplated suicide, you will suffer from job dissatisfaction and a condition aptly called 'burn out'.

"All of you will be chronically depressed."

Ohhh…

"In short, by repetitive grinding as cogs in the American legal system, you will irrevocably come to fully think like a lawyer."

As the Dean droned on about the stress… long hours… sleep deprivation… competitive pressure… social alienation… sense of isolation and loneliness that went with lawyering, Henrietta recalled advice she'd got during a recent visit by Mr. Harold Mixon, once her boss at her little ol' hometown's now defunct weekly newspaper and the only daddy figure she had ever known.

Mr. Harold had also warned that becoming a lawyer would change her way of thinking about things, by upsetting balance between the left side of her brain—said to be handy for logical, analytical, orderly thought—versus the right side—said to be suited for creativity, intuition, and "holistic" mental processing.

"And now for the bad news," the Dean was saying. "Your life expectancy as lawyers will be somewhat longer than that of laypersons, your misery seemingly eternal."

Ohhh…

"That said, I shall depart from reciting rules for you to mindlessly scribble and memorize. Instead, I shall provide instruction in Legal Ethics and Professional Lawyerly Conduct—an oxymoronic subject, many would say—by the Socratic method that mirrors the adversarial system of the

American legal process."

Uh oh.

Henrietta had got the idea of becoming a lawyer from seeing the old movie called *Legally Blonde*. And had also watched the older one called *The Paper Chase*, also set at Harvard Law School. So although the Judge Judy School of Law did not use the so-called Socratic method in a "live" way, she knew how the well educated professors posed situations and peppered uneducated students with questions in relentless slicing-and-dicing of complicated circumstances.

According to the "mirrored" so-called adversarial system, having advocates on opposing sides of a legal dispute go at each other like Pit Bull dogs was the best way of disposing of false notions and getting at truth. Based on her three months of experience as a legal intern in the nearby small-town law office of Willis "V.-for-Versus" Willis, however, in actual practice…

Uh oh again.

"Ms. So-and-So," said the Dean, pointing a finger straight at her own self. "If you pass the bar exam and get a job, it is theoretically possible that you would be allowed to argue a case on appeal in the United States Supreme Court. In that venue, clerks would have read your written brief, independently researched applicable law, and Justices would use you and your oral arguments as props for publicly confirming their already-made decisions. If properly supervised, however, you would by no means be entrusted with a seemingly simple matter at trial in, say, traffic court, for which you would be hopelessly out of your shallow depth."

Ohhh…

"For pedagogical purposes, however, let's assume you are a licensed but unsupervised lawyer presented with the following situation, to-wit:

"A middle-aged mother brings her teenaged son, Johnny Gray, into your office. She says the boy only 'witnessed' an attempted theft of a motor vehicle, but that she fears Johnny might 'become involved' if he reports what he saw to the police.

Would you ask your teenaged client if he had already 'become involved' as something other than an innocent bystander?"

Hmmm.

Not able to recall such an issue coming up in her law school studies—and only approximately in her work as a licensed legal intern—Henrietta reckoned it would be sensible to ask a walk-in client about his possible involvement in a crime he claimed to have witnessed, but—dang it—felt like a chicken about to be ground up in a dance with the devil.

CHAPTER 2

As the strawberry-blonde female beside him continued to dance around Dean Griswold's simple line of questions, R. Marcus Burnham—the recently adopted R standing for nothing—could barely contain himself. "Take it off!" he wanted to scream…not at the dancer, but at the Dean. Had he himself been conducting the cram course, he would have stripped the poser bare of pretense, exposed her lack of legal learning, lashed her mercilessly with scathing put-downs and…

Though he had never been inside the nearby Lady Godiva Cabaret, nor any other so-called "gentlemen's club", inside University of Tulsa Law School classrooms he had witnessed numerous performances of the pathetic routine currently in progress. Too dumb to engage in intellectual give-and-take with professors and male students, members of the unfair sex—obviously admitted by T.U. to satisfy government-mandated "gender equality"… Damnit, one particular teaser—though not a blonde—had brazenly used her T-and-A to jack up her G.P.A. and had already been hired by…

Marcus reminded himself that he was the smartest person in the room.

For the past three years he had spent at least eighteen hours a day either in class, studying into wee hours, or researching complicated legal issues for the *Law Review*. He had graduated at the top, almost, of his class. He would ace the upcoming bar exam without breaking a sweat. And yet… He had signed-up for the otherwise pointless Acheron Academy cram course only to get the attention of Dean Griswold. The Griswold & Griswold firm was among the most prominent in town, but obviously also under DEI pressure to hire only…

"Under no circumstances should 'Miss Legally Blind' expressly ask the teenaged client about his possible involvement in the attempted theft of a motor vehicle!" he shouted in answer to the simple question that the little wannabe barrister was obviously too "blonde" to comprehend, much less intelligently answer.

Ohhh…

"As a lawyer, she is a sworn officer of the court in our system for determining truth and applying justice," Griswold predictably countered. "Why shouldn't she ask Johnny Gray if he was 'involved' in the alleged crime, Mr.… uh, Burnham?"

"Because the client might admit to criminal involvement, might later be charged and put on trial, in which case she, knowing the truth—though bound to maintain confidentiality—would be also bound to not suggest untruth by cross-examination of potential witnesses…"

"I could still cross-examine witnesses to impeach their general credibility!" the little strawberry-blonde barista retorted.

"Nor would she be able to put her client on the stand and standby during what she knew to be perjurious testimony!"

"I likely wouldn't put Johnny Gray on the stand anyway if I found out he had been criminally involved in attempted car theft! How would I deal with a District Attorney if I didn't know what fix the teenager might be in?"

"It's called lawyering," Marcus scoffed. "It's knowing how to get around rules without actually breaking them at risk to oneself."

Ohhh…

"Very well, Mr. Burnham," said the Dean. "Inasmuch as you, I understand, are among the, uh, 'sharpest shooters' in this year's T.U. Law School crop of would-be hired guns, let's suppose you too are an unsupervised lawyer, in the same case; and that the mother of a teenaged Jimmy Black comes into your office and tells you that an old woman who owned the vehicle caught Jimmy along with another boy in the act of attempting to steal it. What would you… ?"

"Aha! Apprised of the alleged facts of the matter, but only by the mother's hearsay that in no way binds me and would be inadmissible at trial for the very reason that it is not necessarily true…"

"Correct regarding admissibility, but not necessarily… "

"I would in turn apprise the client that, under Oklahoma Law, theft of a motor vehicle is a felony that could result in imprisonment for a term of up to five years…"

Oh.

"… that unauthorized use of a vehicle temporarily depriving the vehicle owner of use is also a felony, punishable by up to two years in prison…"

Oh.

"… and with tone-of-voice emphasis, perhaps accompanied by appropriate body language, I would further advise that simple unauthorized use of a motor vehicle a/k/a 'joyriding' is only a misdemeanor, subject to a year of imprisonment but more likely resulting in a fine of not more than five hundred dollars."

Ohhh…

"Remarkable instant partial recall of memorized material, Mr. Burnham. Another lawyer, not familiar with the governing statute, would have had to open a book or use a computer, and would likely have also noted that intent is the factor that distinguishes felonious vehicle theft and unauthorized use from 'joyriding'. But…"

"I have no interest in such petty matters, Dean Griswold. My qualifications and ambitions are to join a prestigious firm and apply myself to important… "

"Yes, but when 'blind' ambition o'er leaps attention to detail…"

"After grilling the client for pertinent factual details and likely receiving an incriminating response, I would contact the District Attorney and steer him toward a determination that my youthful client was only…"

"As I was about to inform you," said Griswold, "an additional factual detail bearing on the case is that the District Attorney had been waging a law-and-order campaign for re-election, pledging to identify and prosecute a local gang of allegedly violent teenagers known as the Killjoyriders."

Ohhh…

"With due respect, Dean Griswold: you should have made me aware of that tangential fact before I might have divulged to the District Attorney…"

"With due disrespect, Mr. Burnham: you should have at least wondered what 'tangential facts' might be in play before divulging, if not more likely asserting to the District Attorney that your client was 'only a joyrider'."

Ohhh…

The devious old "psychopomp" had led him into an ambush, Marcus realized. The class exercise was not about legal ethics and professional conduct, nor about the personal "danger" of passing a bar exam and becoming a "miserable" licensed attorney. Dealing with issues raised by the staged case was all about Dean Virgil Griswold attempting to demonstrate that he himself was the smartest person in the room.

CHAPTER 3

Though spitefully not unhappy about R. Marcus Burnham getting put down a peg, Henrietta was wary as Dean Griswold—like a hunting dog after dropping a dead duck from its jaws—raised his head and scanned the room. Sure enough…

"Back to you, Miss So-and…"

"Ms. Hebert, spelled H-e-b-e-r-t, but pronounced 'Ay-bear' on account of the Cajun nature of the long gone daddy I never knew."

As the Dean flipped the black tassel to the other side of his flat-topped cap, then looked at her like she her own self was some kind of mutt, a past encounter with a notorious high school bully came to mind. Leon Corn—who made a practice of de-pantsing smaller boys and poking fun at the size of their peckers—had that same look in his eyes the moment before she fetched a knee up into his own crotch and set him to squealing like a stuck pig.

"Very well, Ms. Hebert," the current de-pantser finally said, "assuming you too were unaware of the District Attorney's crackdown on a violent teenaged gang of Killjoyriders…"

"Why shouldn't she have expected such a 'tangential' fact might rear its head?" said the class' flaming, uh, redhead.

"…when you contacted the D.A.'s office to find out what kind of 'fix' your client, Johnny Gray, might be in, suppose a talkative clerk told you that a somewhat elderly woman who owned the vehicle in question not only caught Jimmy Black and another teenager in the act of attempting to 'use' her car, but also attacked the would-be thieves with a baseball bat."

Ohhh…

"What, if anything, would you do, and why?"

Hmmm.

Henrietta answered that she would get back to Johnny Gray and outright ask the client if he his own self was a Killjoyrider and/or the "other boy" caught in the act of stealing an old woman's car. 'Cause if a fracas broke out…

"You were told by someone in the D.A.'s office that, in fact, a 'fracas' did break out."

Well then, if the old lady got hurt… Though in fact reckoning she would have told Johnny Gray how the cow ate the cabbage for even just standing by during a fracas involving a semi-elderly woman, Henrietta said she would be sure to remind the client to—for the time being—not tell police or anyone else about what he had witnessed. 'Cause…

"What if told that the 'old' woman was not yet sixty, strong as a horse, and known as the 'Louisville Slugger', not only because of her past on-field prowess as a member of a championship softball team, but because she was an incorrigible barroom brawler with a record of multiple assaults and, heh, heh, 'batteries'?"

Ohhh…

"Criminy, Dean Griswold, you didn't tell me about any of those pertinent facts," the whiner beside her complained. "If I had known about the old biddy's actions and reputation, I would have filed a criminal complaint against her with the District Attorney, and sued her ass in civil court on behalf of my client, young Jimmy Black."

Ohhh…

"Ah, more lawyering raises its ugly head," said the Dean in a disgusted tone of voice. "Japan, with a population of about 125 million people, has only about 40,000 licensed attorneys. Contrary to the law of supply-and-demand, however—when it comes to lawyers, 'tis said the more there are, the greater the need—California's population of about 40 million people is plagued by 175,000 legal finaglers."

"And most of the new ones getting all the good jobs are

females of the species!" R. Marcus Burnham added.

"But I digress," said the cram course instructor, again raising his head to survey the room. "Ms. So-and-So Number Two," he said, eyeing the only other gal present, "let's assume you too are a practicing attorney, engaged to represent the interests of the old woman in this matter, a Ms. Green. Faced with possibilities of both criminal and civil litigation, what would you do?"

"Well, I would not expressly ask Ms. Green if she injured anyone."

"Uh hum."

"Dang it, she's copying my advice to my client," Jimmy Black's lawyer squealed.

"And I would tell her not to talk to police or anyone else about what happened."

"Uh hum."

"Again, Dean Griswold, that's exactly what I advised my client."

"But I would ask her to tell about events leading up to the, uh, fracas, including in particular the actions of that teenaged Killjoyrider represented by Marcus Burnham."

"I object to…to my client being ganged-up on by these members of the unfair sex!"

The Dean said it was understandable that Ms. Green's lawyer would seek justice for her client, and predictable that she would also seek monetary damages in which she, as plaintiff's attorney, would share. But then reminded "Ms. Number Two" she would not yet have known about the possible involvement of Mr. Burnham's client in the fracas, "unless the District Attorney had shared such a suspicion that might have been stirred up by the lawyer for Jimmy Black blundering prematurely into a 'joyrider' line of defense."

Ohhh…

"I didn't 'blunder'! My client's possibly attempted joyriding, even if admitted or proven in court, would not relieve that blonde so-called lawyer's client from liability for assault-and-battery."

"Despite your lawyerly eagerness to also precipitously initiate civil litigation, Mr. Burnham," said the Dean, "in this case you would likely not profit from the misfortunes of others. For in fact, the Louisville Slugger 'struck out' during the fracas resulting from the attempted illegal use of her vehicle. And was later sent to a 'dugout', heh, heh, dead as Casey's nuts."

Ohhh...

"There you go again, baiting-and-switching traps for only me."

Dang it, Henrietta decided that in real life she would not have took on the defense of Johnny Gray, at least not without first being pretty dang sure he had not had a hand in—and maybe not unless satisfied that he had in fact only stood by during—the "heh, heh" death of the oldish Louisville Slugger. But then...a song from the musical version of *Legally Blonde* came to mind:

♫ *Oh dear, I fear my comment has offended/ Hard to argue, though, when you're too mad to speak/ You're employment will be very quickly ended/ When they see how your emotions make you weak...* ♫

CHAPTER 4

Marcus was of two minds. One urged him to continue demonstrating that he—not Dean Virgil Griswold—was the smartest person in the room. The other cautioned him to start sucking-up to the pretentiously self-professed "psychopomp".

According to the Acheron Academy website, the cranky old cram course instructor—scion of the Griswold & Griswold law firm's founding family—had retired from active law practice ten years ago. Probably because he didn't have what it took to win in dog-eat-dog competition with other lawyers. Probably that was why he joined the faculty of the so-called academy. In the pseudo-arena of academia, usually facing only lesser intellects, he could presume to deliver pinheaded 'words of caution' about his betters passing into "Hell".

When faced with someone of superior smarts... Yeah, like members of the T.U. Law School faculty, daunted by the brain power of a particular student, Griswold obviously had his nose out of joint. To retaliate, the bilious old bastard also obviously favored fatuous females such as a certain Ms. Witte, the conniving big-boobed bimbo who had used her feminine assets to impress T.U. Law School professors and finish with top grades. Thanks to so-called DEI and other BS, Ms. "Dimwitte" was among women constituting more than half the class, almost all of whom had already got jobs as law firm associates or government attorneys, while he himself...

Marcus ground his teeth.

Damnit, he could have made himself likable. In law school, he could have joined a collegial study group. He could have shared the fruits of his brilliance and hours of independent study with lazy, weak-minded others. But why? Why would he be helpful to others in cutthroat competition to…

He could have gotten dozens of job offers by now. But to what end? To become a likable but undistinguished paper-shuffler, toiling away in a law firm's boiler room, enabling nominal superiors such as Virgil Griswold to get the credit? No, not him, not R. Marcus Burnham, the smartest person in every room he had ever entered.

As barely a teenager — after seeing an old semi-documentary movie about a famous 1925 trial of a Tennessee high school teacher for teaching evolution in violation of state law — he had adopted the legendary trial attorney, Clarence Darrow, as his role model. Particularly inspiring was the depiction of Darrow's withering cross-examination of opposing counsel — a perennial losing presidential candidate named William Jennings Bryan — that made a monkey of the old Bidenesque politician and directly led to the doddering old man's death. True, in connection with another case Darrow was charged with misconduct, discredited, and disbarred in at least one state, but…

Not long afterward, he'd seen a documentary titled *O.J.: Made in America* featuring famous trial attorney, F. Lee Bailey getting O.J. Simpson off the hook for murder by brilliantly cross-examining a Los Angeles Police Department detective and getting the cop to admit to past utterance of the N-word. Unfortunately, Bailey was also charged with misconduct in another case and was also disbarred, but…

A year or two later, he had been further inspired by tv news accounts of the shakedown of Donald Trump by a lawyer named Michael Avenatti on behalf of a porn star that was the basis of Trump's later conviction on thirty-two felony counts. Hell, Avenatti made one hundred and eight appearances on CNN and MSNBC during a period of sixty days, and was himself prominently mentioned as a viable presidential candidate. True, the combative trial lawyer was now serving a prison sentence for extortion and theft in other cases, but…

Jimmy McGill a/k/a Saul Goodman, attorney in *Breaking Bad* and *Better Call Saul,* who astutely advised that conscience gets expensive…

"Mr. Burnham, are you still with us, or are you in shock to have learned of your client's serious legal peril, for which you are partly responsible?"

Marcus bit his tongue, literally. The hypothetical case put forward and repetitively "tweaked" by Griswold was not worthy of his attention, but…

"Jerry White's disclosure to an attorney makes your gratuitous confession of your client's 'joyriding' hobby look quite stupid."

"I was too bored with this class to listen to what a 'lawyer' for a 'Jerry White' had to say."

"Too bad, not for you but for your client, Jimmy Black. On the other hand, if you had grilled your client—and listened to what he had to say—you might have already known about Jerry White's involvement in the fracas that resulted in the death of an old woman, and…"

"Like I already said, good lawyers don't grill clients for confessions of guilt that might come up later and bite them in the ass."

"To the contrary, Mr. Burnham, if told boring details of the involvement of a third boy—Jerry White—a 'good' lawyer might have foreseen that, to more inquisitive counsel, your client's cohort would likely make self-serving statements, perhaps claiming… Oh, say that Jimmy Black and he were members of the Killjoyriders gang, and that—when the two of them were confronted by an old 'bat', heh, heh—your client asked to be handed a monkey wrench."

"Dean Griswold, please, let's play fair. At the time I first talked to my client, it would have appeared that he was possibly involved, at worst, in attempted theft of a motor vehicle. And that's all Jimmy Black would likely have confessed to. By attempting to set up a reduced charge for misdemeanor joyriding and… and… Regardless of what I did or didn't do, you—as an all-knowing 'psychopoop'—would dredge up 'facts' that incriminated my client instead of 'Jerry White' or…

"What about this strawberry-blondish so-called lawyer's client, 'Johnny Gray', who supposedly just stood by and watched the old woman get the worst of it?"

Aha!

Viciously gratified by sight of a suddenly stricken look in Griswold's usually deadened eyes, Marcus himself "stood by" without pity as the old man then announced a five-minute break and retreated from the basement hellhole.

CHAPTER 5

With Oscar North just setting there like a bump on a log—and both crammers at back-row desks next to him adamantly refusing to switch to her front-row spot—Henrietta debated with her own self whether to wait for Dean Griswold to return from likely relieving hisself or ditch the remainder of the cram course.

On the one hand, as a licensed intern for Willis V. Willis, Esquire, she had already learned about the law most applicable situations such as the one laid out by the Dean. It was called Murphy's Law by Willis, who from almost forty years of experience as a trial lawyer had learned the hard way that, in his words, "the first casualties in the fog of courtroom combat are pre-trial strategies and tactics."

Though still well known in Okmulgee County as the "LitiGator", her boss was now chronically fearful that he his own self, contrary to his advertised reputation, might get "eaten alive" if he dared to again venture into a "hellish" hall of so-called justice. Suffering from what a doctor might've called PTSD, he had took to over-serving hisself with daily doses of spiritous beverages. Due to him being almost always under weather of late, she her own self had had to deal with clients, lawyers, plus judges in occasional courtroom appearances. And from just pre-trial jousting had learned that, sure enough, in the process of adversarial litigation, anything that could go wrong would go wrong.

Hmmm.

On the other hand, she had not had a date since Gus was a

pup, and Oscar North was not too ordinary in the face to look at. By putting up with more contrariness of the old Acheron Academy Dean, not to mention the annoying wiseass attitude of R. Marcus Burnham, she would have a chance to "bump into" the bashful "bump" after class.

Hmmm.

Back to seated in the front row, the redheaded peckerwood perched beside her scooted his desk closer to hers.

"Pssst!" he psssted. "We need to, uh, talk off the record," he semi-whispered, "like lawyers would do in a real case."

Henrietta scooted away, but…the pushy pssstster also kept on scooting, and semi-whispering.

"By positing that 'Jerry White' told another lawyer my client had asked to be handed a monkey wrench during the fracas, Griswold is setting us up to take the fall. Next thing we know, the old would-be psychopomp will…"

"The Dean only said that you should have foresaw a possibility of such turns of events. We our own selves wouldn't know what Jerry White told a lawyer about a monkey wrench. We're in fog."

"Griswold will assign an 'attorney' to represent White, then 'lead' the dummy to contacting the District Attorney and cutting a deal that incriminates…"

"Just like you your own self already did by telling someone at the D.A.'s office that your client, 'Jimmy Black', was a 'just a joyrider' before knowing about the fracas and death of the old Louisville Slugger."

"And just like Griswold will pressure you to do on behalf of your client, 'Johnny Gray', who told you he witnessed the attempted, uh, joyriding."

Hmmm.

In fact, Henrietta had already decided that—if again called on by Dean Griswold, she would do about that very thing: declare to the cranky course instructor that she would try to reach agreement with the District Attorney for her client—and, in return for telling what happened—not have Johnny Gray charged with any criminality. But…

According to R. Marcus Burnham—who was obnoxious but obviously smart as mustard—though "psychopomps" were supposed to be nonjudgemental, the Dean was acting like a an advocate for the devil.

"Like the Fed lawyers who nailed President Trump's attorney for criminal conduct in order to get his former client impeached. And when that didn't get Trump booted from office, like the female District Attorney in New York, who later put screws to Trump's accountant and got convictions for thirty-two bookkeeping misdemeanors that somehow added up to felonies when coupled with minor election law violations.

"Your client, Johnny Gray, could be likewise targeted as a weak link," he said. "Unless we…"

"As far as known—and only to me my own self—Johnny Gray only witnessed two boys trying to possibly steal a car," Henrietta semi-whispered back. "Though that its own self would be helpful to prosecution of your client, we don't know that my client witnessed the fracas, saw anyone hand a monkey wrench to anyone, or could even identify either of the two other teenagers."

"Ha! You think a mother would have dragged her teenaged son into a lawyer's office—and put down a retainer for legal services no doubt amounting to thousands of hard-earned dollars—if she didn't know her bad boy was in deep shit? Try to think like a lawyer."

Hmmm.

Henrietta reckoned that possible legal peril of her client was all the more reason for her own self to go along with "being led" to contact the District Attorney, and make what was called a plea deal for lenient treatment of Johnny Gray for any "involvement", but…

"Jerry White's attorney might astutely advise him not to come forward with information about what did or didn't happen," said Jimmy Black's pushy lawyer. "But regardless of what your client did or didn't tell you, 'someone' might claim that <u>he</u> wielded the monkey wrench that killed the old woman."

Hmmm.

"But say Jerry White gets bad legal advice and takes the risk of coming forward and ratting-out Jimmy Black. If you advised Johnny Gray not to put himself in legal peril, it would be the rat's word against that of my better represented client," said the slippery sumbitch. "Otherwise, well, I might have to cut a deal with the D.A. at your client's expense."

Hmmm.

"So let's teach Griswold a lesson about real lawyering," the would-be lawyer assigned to represent Jimmy Black continued, as from overhead came the sound of a toilet being flushed. "Let's put our heads together in the mutual interest of our respective clients, stand up to Griswold's bullying and thwart the old bastard's attempt to prove he's smarter than… than us."

Hmmm.

To Henrietta, R. Marcus Burnham now sounded not so much like the *Simpsons* blue-haired lawyer as more like the cartoon brat in *Calvin and Hobbes* elementary school books, saying such things as it being hard for a super-genius like hisself to put up with all the idiots in the world, and that some kids—including Einstein—got bad grades in school because classes moved too slow for them. On the other hand, she also recalled the latter cartoon character saying that not enough scientific research was devoted to finding a cure for jerks.

CHAPTER 6

Marcus scooted his desk away from the strawberry-blonde. Damnit, putting their heads together to avoid mutual risk of their clients turning against one another was the obvious play, but Ms. "Aybear" was a dummy. And with Griswold back at the podium…

"Let's review what is known and not known by lawyers representing parties to the situation in our Case of the Killjoyriders," said the manipulative old man, "to-wit:

"Unless divulged by her possible contact with another attorney, perhaps based on a personal relationship, presumably only counsel engaged to represent Johnny Gray would know that he claimed to have only witnessed an attempt by two other boys to illegally 'use' a motor vehicle.

"By way of hasty contact with the District Attorney's office, counsel for Jimmy Black has learned that his client's participation in the escapade was interrupted by an old woman wielding a baseball bat, and — as now also generally known — that a 'fracas' ensued.

"Jerry White has told his lawyer he was in attendance at the fracas and that Jimmy Black asked him to hand over a monkey wrench.

And by now, heirs of Ms. Green have engaged counsel to represent their interests. Everyone else would likely know that the somewhat elderly woman was the vehicle's owner and has died, presumably as a result of injuries inflicted upon her during her involvement in the fracas.

"So let's first consider and dispose of the civil case for monetary damages that counsel for the victim's heirs indicated she would file," said the Dean, pointing a finger at the blonde previously appointed to fill that role. "How would you know whom to sue, Ms.…"

"Meginniss, spelled M-e-g… uh… i-n-n-i-s-s. In answer to your question, I suppose I would sue, uh, like I said before… Jimmy Black?"

"Here we go again, everyone picking on me," said Marcus. "The old bat should have called the cops when she saw her car being monkeyed with, should not have confronted the would-be joyriders, and should not have even threatened use of excessive force with a… with a Louisville Slugger. She had it coming, and…"

Ohhh…

"… with me representing him, Jimmy Black, if charged, would be acquitted of any and all criminal charges against him, except possibly attempted joyriding, a minor misdemeanor."

Ohhh…

"That wouldn't matter in the civil lawsuit," someone on the back row of class piped up to point out. "O.J. Simpson got acquitted on charges of murdering his ex-wife and a fella named Goldman, but then lost a civil case brought against him by the victims' families for causing wrongful deaths. And had a judgement of over 30 million dollars of mostly punitive damages hanging over him for the rest of his life."

"You sir, Mr.…?" said the Dean to the backbencher.

"Oscar North, but everyone always calls me Billy."

"You are quite right, Mr. North. An acquittal on criminal charges — for which the prosecution is required to prove guilt beyond a reasonable doubt — does not relieve a defendant from liability in a civil action that requires proof of wrongdoing by only a preponderance of evidence."

"Everybody knows that," Marcus snorted. "But if Simpson had been represented by F. Lee Bailey in the civil case — like in his criminal trial — he would not have ended up hopelessly in debt for the rest of his life. Bailey would have counter-sued for forty million, and won!"

"You, Mr. North, are hereby appointed to serve as Jerry White's counsel in this matter," Griswold announced.

"Golly, Dean Griswold, I don't want to be anybody's lawyer, ever. I would rather be an undertaker, and bury Ms. Green with a smile on her face. But my father…"

"Don't worry about it, Billy," said Marcus. "You don't have a snowball's chance in hell of passing the bar exam, which is just as well. Unless someone did something stupid," he added, with a warning glance at the strawberry-blonde beside him, "in a showdown between us, it would be my word against yours."

For just a second, another sort of wounded look came into the Dean's eyes, this time directed at Billy North. But a second later…

"I would like to think, Mr. Burnham, that what you mean is that if their respective testimonies came into open conflict, it would be your client's word against that of Mr. North's client," said the so-called Dean of the so-called Acheron Academy in a pointedly skeptical tone of voice. "I would like to believe that you, even in the heat of the moment, would not put your own words into your client's mouth, and thereby suborn perjury."

Ohhh…

"What I mean," said Marcus, "is that in a showdown with North—a known five-time loser—it would be my lawyering against his lawyering, and that I would win."

Booo…

"As put in a musical version of that otherwise dumb movie called *Legally Blonde*, to-wit: 'Only some law students turn out to be sharks, just some/ The rest turn out to be chum.'"

Ohhh…

CHAPTER 7

As Dean Griswold took to browbeating Ms. Meginniss about opening a can of worms, Henrietta stifled an urge to stand up and open a can of sass in his direction, but….

In the words of H.D.C. Pepler," said the blonde gal, "quote: 'The law that lawyers know about is property and land…'"

"If only this case were about 'property and land', Ms. M-e-g-i-n…"

"But 'why faith is more than what one sees/And hope survives the worst disease/And charity is more than these…'"

"Your, or rather Mr. Pepler's point, Ms. M-e…?"

"'Lawyers do not understand.'"

Ohhh…

The class' redheaded snarker snickered. But the red-faced Dean…

"Indeed, Ms. M-e-g-i-n-n-i-s-s, in the more prosaic words of the late Justice Scalia, quote: 'The main business of a lawyer is to take the romance, the mystery, the irony, the ambiguity'—and I would add, the poetry—out of everything he touches.'"

Ohhh…

"Thus, you are excused, my dear," he said with a wave of his hand. "Go in peace, and I will count my time here today as not totally wasted."

Ohhh…

Henrietta got halfway to her own feet, but….

"Now, Ms. Hebert, with threat of distracting civil litigation disposed of, let's return to consideration of your client's involvement in our case. You indicated earlier that you would have asked Johnny Gray if he himself was a would-be 'joyrider' at the time he reportedly 'witnessed' the attempted heisting of a motor vehicle. Presumably not wondering why his mother would see the need to pay for engagement of your services, you seemed to have believed his potential legal peril was of minor misdemeanor magnitude and could be disposed of administratively. But… "

"That is exactly what I tried to tell her during the break," said the class bellyacher. "Innocent 'bystanders' don't rush to hire expensive lawyers!"

"Now that you know that a fracas occurred, and that a somewhat elderly woman died as what appears to have been a result, what would you… ?"

"I dang sure would not put my head together with this here lawyer for Jimmy Black!"

"Heads together?" said the Dean with raised eyebrows.

"Big mistake, Ms. Hebert," said the would-be cooperator. "By betraying a professional confidence and making an enemy of… of my client, you have put your own client in worse legal jeopardy."

Dean Griswold conceded that the sumbitch had made a good point, which took her back a peg. Lawyers were often required to become "strange bedfellows" in the mutual interests of their clients, he said.

Hmmm.

Maybe the Dean also had something against "females" becoming lawyers. Maybe he aimed to also run her own self out of his class, Henrietta was thinking. And then…

As the older, smarter version of Leon Corn turned a hard stare toward Oscar North, she had a little pang of guilty feeling for even listening to R. Marcus Burnham's proposition that she take a side that might be contrary to the interests of the would-be joyrider represented by her obviously not so smart classmate.

"Mr. North, now that you've had time to think about it: told by your client that Jimmy Black had asked him to hand over a monkey wrench," said the big bully, "what would you have done?"

"Well, after knowing—like you said I would—that an old

Ms. Green got killed in a fracas that broke out, I reckon I would have contacted the police and/or the District Attorney about…"

"Really?! Would you not have first asked your client if he in fact handed over a monkey wrench, and—if so—at what point during the incident?"

"Well…"

"If told by Jerry White that he did hand over the potential weapon, would you not have wondered about what expectation if not purpose he had in mind?"

"Well…"

"While respectable opinions may differ about a lawyer directly asking a client if he committed an apparently criminal act, would you not have attempted to determine—before contacting authorities—whether your client even witnessed the assault on Ms. Green?"

"Well…"

"Dumb question," said the class smart aleck. "Even if my client did ask to be handed a wrench for some reason, and someone used the tool as a 'weapon' in the fracas, I would have immediately put the loser wise to his client being in deep dung."

"Indeed, Mr. Burnham, it might have appeared—or been made to appear—that Mr. North's client, even if not the 'someone' who possibly wielded the monkey wrench against Ms. Green, could be found to have been an accessory to the act. But…"

"Golly, Dean Griswold, are there going to be complicated questions like this on the next bar exam?" said Oscar.

Henrietta had been wondering almost the same thing. Why was the Dean's cram course on Professional Ethics and Professional Conduct so focused on issues raised in a particular Killjoyriders case?

"Don't worry about it, Billy," said "Jimmy Black's" mouthy mouthpiece. "Like I said before, no way are you going to pass the exam. But for purposes of this game, I would bail you out by offering to cooperate with you instead of Johnny Gray's female attorney in construction of a stonewall defense for both our clients."

If standing, Henrietta would have stomped a foot and told Oscar North not to…

"In answer to your inquiry, Mr. North, you will indeed be confronted by bar exam questions somewhat such as I have put to you," said the Dean. "But in detached third-person academic form, likely without 'complicated extralegal tactical' angles such as Mr. Burnham has brought into play."

"Phew!" Oscar sighed.

"Were you to pass the exam, however," Griswold continued, "in actual practice you might well be approached by another lawyer such as Mr. Burnham in connection with tactical issues more about what a lawyer <u>would</u> do as opposed to what he-or-she should do in a case such as this."

"I would not be a strange bedfellow with him!"

Ha, ha, ha…

"Why not? Presumably aware that a falling out among thieves was possible, if not virtually inevitable in this case—and that Mr. Burnham would be professionally obliged to at least raise the possibility that 'someone' other than his client might be primarily responsible for the death of Ms. Green—why would you not 'play ball' with him in the interests of… ?"

"I'm just not cut out for lawyering," said Oscar, standing. "I'm going to skip the bar exam this year and be an undertaker," he said, before turning to…

"Wait!" Henrietta hollered. "I would have contacted and, uh, cooperated with you 'stead of with Jimmy Black's shifty shyster!"

Ohhh…

"You'd be sorry!" the shifty shyster hollered back.

Ohhh…

Dean Griswold eyed her with a sorta hurt look, but then…

"Unless there was a personal relationship between the two of you, how would you have known to contact Mr. North?" he hollered at her.

"Well, like I said, I would have grilled my client about what happened and didn't happen, and… With a minute to ponder, I would have reckoned that Johnny Gray—also a teenager—would likely have known or at least recognized Jimmy Black and Jerry White during the attempted heist that he at least witnessed."

Ohhh…

"Easy to say now that you have 'pondered' But very well, Ms. Hebert, assuming Johnny Gray knew and told you what happened—and again, except for perhaps a personal relationship—why would you have potentially deepened your client's involvement in a homicide case by 'cooperating' with Jerry White's or Jimmy Black's attorney?"

"Get in bed with me," said R. Marcus Burnham, scooting his desk back closer to hers. "I'll teach you the facts of life."

"Don't go Oscar!" Henrietta shouted as her targeted date headed for the door. "Stay right here and…"

"Yes, Mr. North, by all means remain with us. With you as his counsel, Jerry White may need the services of an undertaker."

As Dean Griswold glared at her like she had accused him his own self of being a shyster, Henrietta braced herself for a verbal lashing. But then…

Hmmm.

… the look in the old ex-layer's bloodshot eyes changed from angry to sorta sad.

CHAPTER 8

Marcus leaned back in his chair, gratified that the Acheron Academy's Dean had switched to dissing the strawberry-blonde and her boyfriend for being dumb about actual practice in cases like the one posed. But puzzled that the ex-corporate lawyer's "pedagogical" effort on the subject of Legal Ethics and Professional Conduct had been almost all about practicalities of trial lawyer strategies and tactics in a particular situation.

With getting a job recommendation in mind, he'd researched the old man's background. And had found that, according to *Martindale-Hubbel*—once the "Bible" for vetting lawyers' qualifications and still referred to by many—Virgil Griswold had graduated from Harvard College in 1980 and Harvard Law School in 1983… passed an Oklahoma bar exam…went to work at Griswold & Griswold… and seemed to have specialized exclusively in real estate transactions.

So yeah, while boardroom negotiations might have been occasionally contentious, sometimes even civilly litigious, it was virtually inconceivable that Griswold would have personally played an active part in any courtroom proceedings. As for ever taking part in criminal litigation, no way… except maybe in one-off administrative handling of a minor traffic court matter as perhaps a favor to a valued real estate client or personal friend. And yet…

Hmmm.

Odd as it was that the "psychopomp" would pose the "Killjoyrider" scenario for his Academy session, even odder was what seemed to be his personal investment in how the contrived case was being handled by the two-dimwitted crammers assigned to represent "Johnny Gray" and "Jerry White". Obviously exasperated by their failure to appreciate the legal peril faced by their respective clients, the old man had blown his usual cool demeanor and—while taking the strawberry-blonde and class dummy to task—had alluded to "perhaps a personal relationship" at play in the case.

Hmmm.

Even the former boardroom real estate attorney had known and conceded that trial lawyers routinely cooperated with and against one another, which by implication would sometimes require them to get professionally cozy—or crossways—with friends and family in the course of doing their job.

Hmmm.

Also strange was that—according to the Acheron Academy website—Griswold had retired from practice ten years ago at what would have been the height of his career.

Hmmm.

Marcus felt somehow uncomfortable that the self-styled "psychopomp" seemed to have become more evenhanded. He didn't trust the pompous…

"Mr. Burnham, your client, Jimmy Black, seems to be up the proverbial creek without a proverbial paddle, thanks in part to your precipitous admission to the District Attorney that Black was at least present during the fracas that resulted in Ms. Green's demise. Indeed, given that Ms. Hebert seems inclined to 'cooperate' with Mr. North in perceived mutual interest of their clients, one might view your canoe as in imminent danger of being sunk. What would you do under such circumstances?"

"One or the other would come around when, uh, Jimmy Black's lawyer applied pressure."

Griswold visibly winced.

"Billy is too dumb to do the math, as anyone would immediately see. But…"

Booo…

"…to Ms. Hebert I would simply point out that two against

one…"

Booo…

"Ms. Hebert appears to more likely become part of a 'two' with Jimmy White's counsel in the scenario I hypothetically propose."

"Billy is obviously a zero, or even a minus-one; likely to incriminate his own client by dumb lawyering. And like I say, when put under pressure, Ms. Hebert would advise her client to, uh, 'reconsider'…"

"Not if my client saw something that might incriminate your client for…"

"… rather than risk subjecting Gray to my cross-examination that would incriminate him."

"Yes! A careful examination of her client's initial account in light of later developments would be her responsibility as counsel for Johnny Gray," his own inquisitor emphatically agreed. But as the cranky old fogey then went back to harassing the female wannabe lawyer… Marcus flashed on Griswold's pedagogical performance as oddly similar to the shtick of T.U.'s also aged, equally dogged Professor Edward "Wrong Way" Williams.

At annual class Christmas parties, the Constitutional Law expert served tap water and popcorn. In class, he crammed Supreme Court decisions down the throats of captive students, along with heaping dishes of his own dissenting opinions. Williams had literally written the book, knew the selected cases inside and out, and for decades had used students as punching bags for exercise of his muscled-up brain. Seemingly obsessed with repetitively proving to his own satisfaction that he would not have made the mistakes he attributed to others, Professor "Wrong Way" even more insanely seemed to think he—by relentless classroom re-litigation—could change outcomes of long-settled cases.

Hmmm.

Maybe Griswold had a grudge, not against him personally, but against trial lawyers in general. What a fool. Without courtroom representation, grievances would not be redressed.

Yes, despite the landmark 1992 lawsuit against McDonald's for serving hot coffee in paper cups, other headlined civil actions had been questionably deemed legally frivolous, notably including the one filed against a dry cleaner in 2005 for failure to pay a customer for losing a pair of pants in violation of "satisfaction guaranteed" advertising… another unsuccessfully waged in 2023 by kidnappers of Lady Gaga's French bulldog for payment of a $500,000 reward… and just last year, an attempt by the family of a deceased swimmer to establish Sea World liability for making a killer whale seem friendly.

But while judges made nuanced interpretations of law, trial lawyers were effectively a fourth and most effective policy-setting branch of government. If not for class-action lawsuits in particular—promoted and funded by trial lawyers who dared to enter the arena of risky litigation—kids would be breathing-in cigarette smoke and asbestos fibers, swimming in oily Alaskan and Gulf of Mexico waters, suffering sexual abuse at Catholic churches and Boy Scout camp-outs. If not for successful class-action litigation in *Jensen v. Eveleth Taconic Company*, sexual harassment of females in the workplace would be unimpeded.

"… and before making an enemy of Jimmy Black's lawyer," Griswold was now saying to the strawberry-blonde, "would you not have worried that he—in defense of his client—might incriminate your client, Johnny Gray?"

"Exactly what I tried to tell her, Dean Griswold," said Marcus. "'Read your Thomas Hobbes,' the *Legally Blonde* musical lyric advises, probably referring to the famous cartoon character—co-founder of the club called G.R.O.S.S. for 'Get Rid of Slimy Girls'—but possibly to the famous English philosopher of the same name who—long before Darwin—observed that the natural condition of mankind is everyone against everyone."

Ohhh…

CHAPTER 9

🎵 *Our topic is blood in the water, kids/ It's time you faced law school is a waste/ unless you acquire a taste/ for blood in the water...* 🎵

With the song from the *Legally Blonde* movie brought back to mind by R. Marcus Burnham's comment about its lyrics, Henrietta had a notion that she her own self had got a bad taste of what it would have been like to attend a real-life law school.

🎵 *You're nothing until/the thrill of the kill/ becomes your only law...* 🎵

To show for the experience, however, she had jotted hardly any notes about law that would be helpful to her passing a bar exam, and not just because she was a left-hander awkwardly stuck in a right-handed high school desk. While slicing-and-dicing only a few legal issues, the Dean had sure enough ground-up practicalities of trial lawyering in the Killjoyriders case, and fed nuggets to the "faces and souls of the heatseekers who had dared to dance with the devil."

But even as to practicalities, if a mother had in fact dragged a teenaged Johnny Gray into the office of Willis V. Willis...

"Like it or not, Ms. Hebert, the fates of three teenaged boys would likely depend on you," said the Dean. "Specifically, regarding the question of whether or not to cooperate with attorneys representing Jimmy Black and/or Jerry White, what would you...?"

"Dang it, Dean, you your own self said that only I my own self would have known Johnny Gray witnessed the attempted, uh, illegal use of Ms. Green's vehicle."

"At the outset, yes, but if either or both attorneys eventually contacted you—presumably based on information provided by their respective clients—would that not indicate that Johnny Gray had likely been not merely a witness, but perhaps a lookout if not otherwise an active participant in the attempted 'joyride' gone awry?"

Hmmm.

"I daresay you would have opened a book or gone online to research applicable law, and would have found…"

"To repeat, Dean Griswold," said R. Marcus Burnham, "I myself would have already known that my client's attempted theft or unauthorized use of a motor vehicle would be a felony, but that attempted use with intent to joyride was only a misdemeanor."

"And I daresay, Ms. Hebert, that you would have also been 'reminded' that under Oklahoma's felony murder statute…"

"I would have known all about that too," said the redheaded know-it-all. "If a death occurs during commission of a felony, regardless of no intent to kill, all the criminal participants can be prosecuted for murder. That's why I would have 'hastily not blundered' by immediately seeking a plea deal for Jimmy Black."

Hmmm.

"Then your client would have had to confide that 'someone' at least threatened to bring a monkey wrench into play, Mr. Burnham. For if you had researched the issue you would have found that the Oklahoma felony murder statute applies only to specific felonies, including robbery with a dangerous weapon."

Hmmm.

"Understanding that Johnny Gray was in peril of being charged with felony murder, Ms. Hebert, I daresay you would have felt intense pressure to cooperate with either counsel for Jimmy Black or counsel for Jerry White before they—as previously suggested by Mr. Burnham—'cooperated' with one another at your client's expense."

Under pressure to take a stand, all Henrietta could think to say was that she'd druther cooperate with the District Attorney and have Johnny Gray tell the truth that at least partly excused him for his possible role in what happened.

"And I would 'druther' have become a major league baseball player instead of a lawyer," the Dean replied. "But you, Ms. Hebert, having hastily taken on Johnny Gray's representation despite your inexperience in criminal trial practice, would have made your bed."

Ohhh…

"What would you do or not do when the bedbugs began to bite?"

Hmmm.

Henrietta in fact began to squirm. Looking over at Oscar North, and him looking back at her with a blankish stare…

"Though Jerry White could be lying, based on him telling that Jimmy Black had asked him to hand over a monkey wrench… I reckon I would put heads together with Oscar."

"Without even wondering why Jerry White was holding a monkey wrench in the first place?!" said the Dean in a semi-desperate tone of voice. "Without checking and perhaps finding that while Jerry White was a known thug, Jimmy Black was a relatively 'good' boy?!"

Ohhh…

"What if you did contact the District Attorney, Ms. Hebert. What if you found that the D.A. had already targeted Jerry White as the poster boy for his anti-joyriding campaign, and that Mr. Burnham's hasty effort to reach a plea deal for Jimmy Black had proven to be fortuitous?"

Ohhh…

"What if the D.A. also offered to Johnny Gray a plea of misdemeanor joyriding in return for his testimony?"

Ohhh…

"Thank you for, uh, endorsing my strategy in this matter, Dean Griswold," said the redheaded brown-noser. "And by the way, I have not yet accepted an offer to…"

"You would be bound to convey any such offer to your client, Ms. Hebert. Would you not be also bound to advise Johnny Gray to consider assisting the District Attorney's prosecution of Jimmy White in return for escaping a potential murder charge?"

the Dean asked, with a downright pleading look in his eyes.

♫Oh dear, I fear my comment has offended/ Hard to argue, though, when you're too mad to speak/ Your employment will be quickly ended/ when they see how your emotions make you weak... ♫

"Alright, dang it, maybe I would have held my nose and gone along with Mr. Burnham's 'fortuitous strategy'," said Henrietta, despite another little pang of guilt about taking a side against Oscar North's client. "But I wouldn't call it 'getting in bed' with him 'stead of, uh, Jerry White's lawyer."

Ha, ha, ha...

As most others again laughed at the phraseology introduced by Dean Griswold, the old Dean hisself slumped his shoulders. But then, with a semi-relieved look in his bloodshot eyes...

"In closing,"he said to no one in particular, "a final word of advice: If you cross into that place of woe and eternal pain among those who are morally neutral opportunists that take either side as theirs, neither in Hell or out of it, constantly stung by guilty conscience and remorse — which is to say, if you become licensed to practice law — do not mistake your license for competence in matters beyond your depth. As the saying goes, he who knows not but knows not he knows not is a fool."

Ohhh...

"In other less prosaic words — those of the noted poet, W.H. Auden — quote: 'If we should weep when clowns put on their show/ If we should stumble when musicians play/ Time will say nothing but I told you so.' Class dismissed."

As other crammers filed out of the basement, Henrietta — semi-stung to have semi-rightly been semi-called "morally neutral" — decided not to latch onto Oscar North. Instead, she went up to the platform, where Dean Griswold still stood behind a podium, now looking down at R. Marcus Burnham and...

"No, I will not 'put in a word' for you!" he barked. "You are a menace to mankind, Mr. Burnham."

As the redheaded Pit Bull puppy scurried away with tail between his legs, she her own self, though fearful of getting bit...

"In a real case, what do you reckon would have likely happened to three teenaged boys whose fates depended on my own self?" Henrietta asked.

"Your cooperation with a District Attorney would likely not have mattered," the Dean only growled. But then, in a gentler tone, "You simply confirmed the practicalities of criminal defense lawyering."

Simply confirmed?

Dean Griswold went on and told that eleven years ago—in semi-connection with a clamor for lenient re-sentencing of prison inmates to align with newly enacted laws—a group of Tulsa University Law School students had looked into a case similar to the one about the Killjoyriders. And found overlooked evidence that "Jerry White" was not the person most responsible for the death of an old woman.

"The findings came too late," he said with a sigh fit for a funeral. "In prison, serving a twenty-five-year sentence for second-degree murder, 'Jerry White' had hanged himself by then."

Dang!

"Who was the most…?"

"Jimmy Black was the Killjoyrider who wielded a monkey wrench against a 'Ms. Green' during the attempted car theft, but had already served a months-long sentence for attempted joyriding and was immune from further prosecution."

"What happened to the sumbitch who got 'Jimmy Black' off by, uh, also cooperating with the D.A. against 'Jerry White'?"

"He's still an active trial lawyer, more successful than ever by all accounts. You've probably seen his billboard signs, advertising that 'Just because you did it doesn't mean they can prove it'."

"Dang it, what about the lawyer for 'Johnny Gray'? You assigned the job to me, then badgered me to go along with…"

"Don't trouble yourself'," said the Dean, stuffing papers into a briefcase. "You only did what circumstances required you to do."

Dang!

"But take my further 'older-and-wiser' lawyer's advice, Ms. Hebert," said the elderly psychopomp. "If you take the bar exam

and become an attorney, limit yourself to a bloodless civil law field of practice involving, say, real estate transactions."
THE
END

CUTTING & PASTING

BIBLE SALESMAN PITCH
"Do… Do… Do you… you…
you want to buy… buy… buy one,
or would you rather have me…
me… me read… read it to you?"

William Danner

SIMON PLASTER

CHAPTER 1

♫Well, I woke up Sunday morning with no way to hold my head that didn't hurt/ Then I fumbled through my clothes and found my cleanest dirty skirt… ♫

Feeling just like the gal singing the old Johnny Cash song last night at the local Bushwhackers honky-tonk, Henrietta left a note on a kitchen table for Bud—a wannabe cowboy she had, uh, danced with last night—then semi-stumbled out the backdoor of the little ol' Trudgeon Street house she had recently come home to.

♫On the Sunday morning sidewalks, wishing, Lord, that I was stoned/ 'Cause there's something in a Sunday, makes a body feel alone… ♫

At the wheel of her old Checker cab of a car, she headed out to meet the day in the little ol' town she had been named for: Henryetta, Oklahoma, advertised on its water tower as "Home of Troy Aikman and Gaylord Goodheart": local boys who both went on to be famous quarterbacks for the Dallas Cowboys.

♫I lit my first and watched a kid cussin' at a can that he was kicking/ And it took me back to somethin' that I'd lost somehow, somewhere along the way… ♫

Back in high school, Gaylord and she had regularly "danced" like two rabbits in a gunny sack. Now, over ten years after he gave her the mitten—her mother's old-fashioned term for being rejected by the one you wanted—well, she still had an empty spot inside herself. Even though Gaylie had turned out to be in fact gay as a flower garden and was now married to a Dallas Cowboy teammate, he would always be the love of her life. Not because she was too old find another; her mother, Wynona Sue had recently found a new love of her own life.

But she her own self, after having boyfriends during the past ten years who said they were crazy about her, had discovered that the love feeling was in the loving, not the being loved. If romance was religion, she reckoned she might as well become a nun in a monastery and keep the feeling alive by prayer and contemplation.

♫*And there's nothin' short of dyin' half as lonesome as the sound/ On the sleeping sidewalks, Sunday morning comin' down…* ♫

Semi-surprised that the Checker had took her to the local high school, Henrietta parked the old car next to the only other one in the otherwise deserted lot. The place where she had first met Gaylie would be empty and locked tight as a wet boot, she knew as she nevertheless walked toward the front entrance of the two-story brick building.

♫*Somewhere far away a lonely bell was ringin'/ And it echoed through the canyons like the disappearing dreams of yesterday…* ♫

Without bothering to try the door, she pressed her face against a glass panel off to the side and… "Well, I declare," Henrietta muttered, as shuffling down a hallway toward her like a gray ghost…

"Is that you your own self, Mr. Bradley?" she exclaimed after her eleventh-grade History teacher—who was already old as hills fifteen years ago—put down a large cardboard box and opened the door.

"It's me, Henrietta—now spelled with an i instead of a y—and Hebert; spelled H-e-b-e-r-t but properly pronounced 'Aybear' on account of my long-gone daddy's Cajun nature. My mother, Wynona Sue…"

"Oh yes, your mother. I well remember…"

"I tried-out for the part of the gal who couldn't say no in the *Oklahoma* musical play you supervised. Wynona Sue came along to help you decide, but… Anyway, I thought that by now you would be, uh, out to pasture."

"I did retire, if that's what you mean," said the old codger, stooping to pick up the cardboard box. "But after the wife passed on," he continued after getting back to upright, "well, I was lonesome for company, and when the high school found itself shorthanded I agreed to step into the breach."

Mr. Bradley let out a mournful sigh and said, "The world has changed since you were in high school, Marietta. The Oklahoma Supreme Court seems to have said that Bibles in classrooms violate the separation of church and state clauses of both state and federal Constitutions, and now—as though Bibles were WMDs—I'm being hauled into court for breaking the law and violating rights of others not to be exposed to 'radiation'."

The aged high school teacher went on to explain that for bringing a Bible into his classroom he was in danger of losing his pension and going bankrupt, if not to jail.

In response to her advice that he needed to hire a lawyer, the poor old man said he had already paid more than he could afford to an attorney who had promised to get his legal troubles settled, but no longer answered his calls. And a trial was set for tomorrow at the Okmulgee County Courthouse.

Henrietta stomped a foot.

Dang it, starting in high school she had set out to expose wrongful doing as a newspaper reporter. After studying-up on Journalism at the Oklahoma Public Education Center under a Professor Owen Hatteras, however—and seeing how dishonest her chosen profession had become—she had tried to set up shop as a private detective while towing repossessed vehicles at night for a bail bondsman in Oklahoma City, but had not had any clients ask for helpful investigations. Until recently, she had worked at odd jobs out in New Mexico to pay for online college and law school education. And now, though her grammar was still inclined to jump fences…

"Wynona Sue finally got another man to marry her, Mr. Bradley. A banjo player in a traveling country-and-western band by the coincidental name of Barney Pickens. So your luck…"

"I made it clear to your mother that I was a happily married man at the time, and would have made it clear more recently that

I was a happily widowed man."

"What I meant by you being in luck was that, well, it was Wynona Sue moving out of the Trudgeon Street house that brought me back to these parts, where I am currently employed as a licensed legal associate of Mr. Willis V. Willis, Esquire. His office is up the road in Okmulgee, right across the street from the county courthouse."

"Mr. Willis is already, or was already my attorney," said her ex-teacher, sidling sideways like a Betsy bug trying to get around a peckish guinea hen.

"Well, you see, Willis has lately been what you might call under weather," Henrietta explained. "But I my own self already have experience about Bibles-in-school cases dating back to my time at OPEC in Oklahoma City, and am available to... ."

"Like I say, Miss, uh, Hebert, I can't afford a lawyer. And now see that I don't need one. The fact of the matter is that I did have a Bible in a schoolroom. As a matter of Constitutional law, I am guilty as charged."

Henrietta stomped her other foot. If there was anything in particular she had learned from her legal studies to date, it was that when the bullshit got stripped away, matters that got brought into court were almost always not in line with what was alleged.

CHAPTER 2

Judge Timothy "T-P" Dwight was a firm albeit selective believer in the divine truth of the Bible, in particular as written in the *Book of Mark*, Chapter 2, Verse 27, to-wit: "The Sabbath was made for man, not man for the Sabbath."

As a matter of faith, not conscious theology, he had long made a practice of devoutly seeking communion with the Almighty, not just in church on Sundays but at every opportunity. And a few years ago — thanks to research by his law clerk --had come to realize that he was not just a Presbyterian, but at heart what was called a "Pantheist": a believer that God was present in all natural things. Today his prayers for oneness with the universe...

"You're in the zone, Two-Putt," his friend, Rich Hughes, confirmed from beside him in the golf cart he drove along the seventh hole of the local country club golf course. "Six bogeys in a row. Keep it up and you'll..."

"Don't jinx me!" T-P barked. Yes, he was only six strokes over par after six completed holes of play, and had hit a long drive right down the middle from the seventh tee. Today could be the day he finally completed an eighteen-hole round in under one hundred strokes, but... God didn't like being taken for granted, and only grudgingly handed out holy grails. Natural things — wind, water, trees, rocks, sand — had a way of thwarting communion. God demanded humility, and golf was rightly known as the most humbling of human experiences.

With the cart brought to a stop, Rich — a Catholic churchgoer who had attended services yesterday — cheerfully wandered into a patch of high weeds in search of his ball. His longtime playing partner—obviously a believer in Biblical verses to the effect that the Sabbath was supposed to be simply a day of rest and relaxation—would never be among the "chosen" elite of only about fifty percent of golfers who ever broke a hundred. For all his routine observance of rituals, his friend would likely never have a truly religious experience.

Not that rest, relaxation and recreation were not important, especially for judges such as himself. Benchwork used to be simple, cut-and-dried, even boring. Heck, he used to doze during trials while lawyers tediously questioned witnesses about meaningless minutiae in attempts to convince jurors of facts of matters. From his presiding perch—as opposed to that of an appellate court judge—he had seldom been required to delve deep into complicated matters of law that his clerk couldn't sort-out on her own.

But nowadays, damnit, everything was legally and politically contentious. Now lower court judges such as himself were increasingly called upon to make decisions about issues that should have been clearly dealt with by the legislative and executive branches of government and/or settled out of court by parties involved in vexing litigation.

Two-Putt sighed.

He had neither the patience nor interest to be a legal scholar. Truth be told, after bouncing from college to college into law school, he had barely met the requirements for graduation. And had first run for election to the non-partisan position of District Judge for Okmulgee County due to lack of success as a practicing attorney, not in but out of court. Put simply, he'd had too few clients to make a living. Now he was paying the price for choosing to spend his workdays in what he'd thought would always be a warm tub of butter.

Out of the cart… standing over his ball with a five iron in hand…he eyed the seventh green seductively lying approximately a hundred-and-fifty yards in the distance. To the left of the putting surface, a pond invited disaster. To the right, a large sand trap warned that escape would cost multiple strokes on his scorecard. A shot that went over the green would put his ball in a clump of trees.

Hmmm.

He'd landed a ball onto a putting surface in so-called "regulation" only once, but damnit… Afterward he had adopted the "Rule" for which he had become known. Given that two putts was the norm, to not waste time—and incidentally, to potentially save strokes—he now made a practice of picking up his ball after getting it onto greens, and carding what would have been the normal results.

So the smart play under current circumstances would be to safely advance his current ball up the fairway, invoke the two-putt rule… chip onto the putting surface with a third shot… record another bogey and move on to his ultimate eighteen-hole goal. But…today, yes, he was "in the zone".

With bated breath and a silent prayer…

Whoosh!

Oh… my… God!

He'd heard that hitting a golf ball in the so-called "sweet spot" of a club face was like sex, only better, but until now… As the tiny white dot soared into a pure blue sky straight for the green, Two-Putt fell to his knees, feeling blissfully at one with the surrounding water… trees… rocks… sand… and everything else in the whole universe.

"Nice shot," said Richie, returned from weedy wilderness after taking three swings to get his ball onto the fairway. "That's a par under your Two-Putt Rule."

Par?! No way. His ball looked to be not more than ten feet from the flag stick, indicating a very makable one-putt—with little or no risk—for a birdie!

T-P ran to the cart… looked at his scorecard… and did the math: with a three on this hole and, say, bogeys on the next two, he would finish the front nine with a score of forty-three! Even if he played the back nine in his usual mid-fifties range… Praise the Lord! He would break a hundred with room to spare!

Leaving his playing partner behind, he drove at top speed

toward the green, thankful to God for his surprising good fortune.

Skidded to a halt at greenside, he grabbed his near-virgin putter and… What in hell? A gaggle of trespassers appeared from behind nearby trees, all wearing ski masks!

One of them commenced to shovel sand from the trap onto the putting surface. Another one turned on sprinklers to flood the green, while a third anti-religious hooligan turned on the large fan designed to dry it out after a soaking rain. As he himself stood there in shock, as though buffeted by a torrential storm…

"The *Book of Luke* tells us that Jesus said: "Woe to you who are rich, for you have received your consolation,' said a fourth intruder, holding what looked to be a Bible.

"I'm not rich," Two-Putt protested. "I am an underpaid public servant, out here in Nature, communing with…"

"'Woe to you who are full now, for you will be hungry.'"

"I had only a glass of orange juice for breakfast, and a small muffin."

"The Bible further tells us that the Lord said unto Moses: 'Hew these two tablets of stone, and I will write upon them the words on the first tablets, which you broke.' And the fourth of God's Ten Commandments etched in stone was this: 'Observe the Sabbath, to keep it holy.'"

Two-Putt dropped both jaw and putter, but…

"We're coming for you, Dwight. Make a wrong decision and you won't know what hit you!" the spokesman for the gang of masked vandals shouted, before leading his cohorts back into the trees.

Drenched—not to mention, rattled—T-P left his putter in a pile of wet sand and hustled back to the cart. Determined to stand firm in the masked face of threats to his Constitutional right to commune with the Almighty as he saw fit… he applied the Two-Putt Rule… and penciled a 4 onto his scorecard.

CHAPTER 3

♫Dropkick me, Jesus, through the goal posts of life/ End over end, neither left nor to right... ♫

With a Sunday song loudly playing on the C&W station of her mother's old radio, Henrietta found Bud—her dance partner from last night at Bushwhackers honky-tonk—setting at the kitchen table in his undershorts, drinking beer from a bottle.

♫Make me, oh, make me, Lord, more than I am/ Make me a piece in Your master game plan... ♫

"Dang it, Henrietta, I reckoned you'd got up and about so early to go get sausage-and-egg biscuits at McDonald's," he said, seeing that she'd returned empty handed. "There's nothin' but beer in the icebox."

♫Free from the earthly tempestion below/ I've got the will, Lord, if You got the toe... ♫

Henrietta stomped a foot... told the wannabe cowboy to saddle up... to go get breakfast for his own self.... and to turn off the radio on his way out.

Set down at the table, she opened her laptop computer and commenced to research issues likely to come up in tomorrow's trial of poor old Mr. Bradley; hauled into court by an outfit called Church of the Open Hand LLC on behalf of members contending that that their Constitutional rights had been violated by the high school teacher having a Bible at school in contrariness to the the separation of church and state rule.

As a Journalism intern for a Professor Hatteras at the Oklahoma Public Education Center some years ago, she had done similar research for a court trial also about a Bible—or part of one—that popped up inside an OPEC classroom. In that case a Phys Ed coach and part-time teacher of English Literature named Joe Dokes had got hisself in trouble by putting the *Genesis I* story of Creation on a reading list for students. Only because he reckoned it was the first story put down in writing, not because he'd ever read it, nor a *Wife of Bath's Tale* neither.

In the end it turned out that Hatteras was a conniving sumbitch in cahoots with the American Civil Liberties Union, and had staged Joe's show trial as a bait-and-switch to settle a personal grudge against the District Attorney. But in the process, Joe—who had never been religious—got around to reading the *Genesis I* story. And, dang it, after marveling about how close the Bible's ancient "metaphoric" description of the world's creation tracked the facts of what modern science later had to say on the subject, admitted on the courtroom witness stand that he was in fact guilty of teaching about religion.

♫**Straight through the heart of them righteous uprights/ Dropkick me...** ♫

Left to her own self, Henrietta—determined to not let Mr. Bradley make the same mistake Joe Dokes made—went to Googling... and right away found that during most of American history, religious instruction had been an ordinary R right along with reading, 'riting and 'rithmatic. Not 'til 1962 did the U.S. Supreme Court decide that mandatory student recitation of prayers in public schools violated the "separation of church and state clause" of the Constitution, which broke a dam for a flood of lawsuits supported by the American Civil Liberties Union.

Including a legal complaint by a mother in Baltimore, Maryland, named Madalyn Murray McNair, who also objected to both Pledges of Allegiance and Bible readings in class. She was an admitted Communist atheist, but got turned away from moving to the Soviet Union, and reportedly told her own young son that in the alternative they would have to "change America", which her lawsuit in fact did. For her tombstone, she said she wanted only three words etched: "Woman. Atheist. Anarchist".

Hmmm.

Next, Henrietta found a 2025 article from a magazine called *Vanity Fair* headlined **How Oklahoma's Right-Wing Superintendent Set Off Holy War in Classrooms**… and read:

Sometimes, Jakob Topper teaches his Christian faith to his six-year-old daughter using children's Bible stories illustrated with teddy bears. Other days, he might use her kid-friendly Bible featuring Precious Moments figures as characters. One thing he knows for sure: The King James version is not on the reading list, given some of its adult themes of sexual assault and incest.

As a parent and a Baptist pastor, Topper opposes Oklahoma's state superintendent of public instruction's mandate to put a King James version Bible in every grade 5–12 classroom.

Hmmm.

Biblical scholars from the University of Oklahoma and elsewhere believe thesuperintendent's standards promote the longstanding trope of white Christian nationalism, which is premised in part on the false idea that the nation's founding documents stemmed from the Bible. For instance, the proposed standards would require students in first grade to learn about David and Goliath, as well as Moses and the Ten Commandments, because the standards cite them as influences on American colonists, Founders, and culture, including the teachings of Jesus of Nazareth (e.g. the 'Golden Rule', the Sermon on the Mount').

Hmmm.

Another posted piece was headlined **Oklahoma Supreme Court Blocks Bible Purchases**, and reported that the State Superintendent of Education had sought to purchase 55,000 Bibles—each containing a copy of the Declaration of Independence and the U.S. Constitution—for use in public schools across the state, at a cost of approximately $3 million in public funds. But the Oklahoma Supreme Court had declared…

At the sound of a key rattling in the front door lock, Henrietta bolted out of her chair. Dang it, she'd not gave an invitation nor hardware for Bud nor anyone else to walk in on her, but…

What in tarnation! Into the living room came none other than her mother, Wynona Sue, followed by a heavy-set, red-faced man loaded down with luggage.

"This here is Orville McCarthy, my new fiancé," said Wynona Sue. "And that there is Henrietta, who now spells her name with an i instead of a y."

"Well, I declare," said the new fiancé, grinning like a sticky-tongued frog in a fly-filled feed lot for cattle. "You two sisters sure enough do look like twins."

"Orville is a very successful door-to-door Bible salesman," her mother announced, "with a big house out in Green Valley, Arizona, and to boot, a country club membership for high-class social activity."

Disappointed that Wynona Sue looked to have not, after all, found a love of her life in Barney Pickens, the banjo player, Henrietta glanced at her watch and told that she was running late for church attendance and didn't have time to chew the fat, or buy a Bible.

"We'll go with you," said her "sisterly" mother, who had likely not set foot in a church even once in the "official thirty-nine years" of her whole life. "Jesus people like to have family Bibles—with the s-e-x parts cut out—for set-about decor. And Orville's got a load of 'em in the back of his vintage Oldsmobile station wagon."

Hoping that Wynona Sue's new fiancé would not embarrass hisself and Wynona Sue—not to mention her own self—during religious services, Henrietta reckoned she might as well actually go to the Church of the Open Hand and hear what its litigious preacher had to say.

CHAPTER 4

♫**You could ride a unicorn to school/ And if you fall off you'd have healthcare (No you don't)...** ♫

As an also red-robed choir sang his selected opening hymn—*Rich, Straight White Men* by Kesha—Reverend Roger Robinson sat in an also on-stage high-backed chair, looking down upon the motley assemblage of troubled souls comprising the congregation of his Church of the Open Hand.

♫**And if you finish school you'd go to college for free/ That makes sense and that's fair (No it's not)...** ♫

Members of the homeless community...the persecuted LGBTQ community... the impoverished Black and Hispanic communities...were prominently sprinkled like salt in the well deserved wounds of the majority in attendance, all well-to-do straight white people.

♫**And if you were a lady, then you own your lady parts/ Just like a man who goes to a dealership and then owns a car (Vroom Vroom)...** ♫

The majority were all self-described "progressives"...successors to the "wealthy woke" of recent years...the "latte liberals" of a few years earlier... and the "radical chic elite" of the 1970s. All were present to indulge in display of their luxury beliefs... their virtue signaling... their shame and guilt for enjoyment of wealth and attendant privilege bestowed upon them by the evil Empire.

♫**If you're from another land and come here/ You won't have to climb a wall (Yes you will)...** ♫

All of them were self righteous types who either drove battery-powered vehicles or bought carbon credits to excuse their destruction of the planet by use of big gas-guzzling cars and private jets, much like medieval churchgoers once purchased Indulgences to avoid punishment for sins. And all were lubriciously eager to be taken to task... to be severely chastised... to be verbally lashed for being superior to the less deserving.

♫**What if rich, white men didn't rule the world any more? Didn't rule the world any more? Didn't rule the world anymore? (Ha, ha, ha, ha, ha, ha, ha)...** ♫

All were sheep, in need of constant shepherding lest they be led astray by right-wing agents of the Empire presuming to use the Bible for their unholy political purposes.

♫**What if...** ♫

With his wife, Sister Sharon, looking up to him from a front-row pew with eyes already enflamed, Roger rose... ran a hand through his head of flaming-red curly hair... spread his arms wide... and to his adoring followers bellowed: "Welcome, one and all who have come to hear me 'talk the talk', heh, heh. Special welcome to those few of you who 'walked the walk' with me earlier this morning."

Attendees looked left and right, most no doubt enviously wondering who among them had been singled out as elitest of the elite.

"But before my delivery of this week's 'What Would Jesus Do?' sermon," he continued, moving to the podium, then raising his personally edited version of the New Testament above his head, "a brief preamble that bears repeating:"

For the benefit of those — most, no doubt — who had not yet fully appreciated his *bona fides* as a seminary graduate and holder of a PhD, Roger yet again explained that the original "good book" was what they, as common people, would understand as a scrapbook of sorts. More accurately described by scholars such as himself as a commonplace book, the original New Testament was a collection of cut-and-pasted materials — most notably including transcripts of four previously oral-only biographies of Jesus attributed to persons known as Matthew, Mark, Luke and John — put down in writing decades after the facts of the matter.

"Abridged wholesome family editions available for only $39.95, bound in leopardskin covers," someone irreverently shouted. "Personally autographed by Marjorie Taylor Greene…"

"Today, for instance, mismarks Jesus' arrival in Jerusalem as 'Palm Sunday' based on the erroneous account in *John* 12:13 that, quote: 'people took branches of palm trees, and went out to meet him,'" Roger continued. "In fact, palm fronds were unavailable in Jerusalem. More to the point, waving of palm branches would have signified triumph, while in fact the Crucifixion that followed was a defeat of Christianity at the hands of the Empire."

Ohhh… the congregation moaned.

"Be not troubled by your inability to grasp the profound truths confounded by errors in standard versions of the Bible," he advised his flock of unversed lay persons. "Each of the four so-called Gospels contained within the standard Biblical canon was written by a different author, each in a different place and time, each from particular point of view. And there are many inconsistencies in the four accounts that—to be understood by ordinary people—require expert 'cutting-and-pasting', heh, heh, by erudite scholars such as myself. Take for instance…"

"Written in simple English, with cartoon illustrations easy to understand as the funny papers…"

"Take for instance the so-called 'Beatitudes' delivered by Jesus to His disciples, on a mount according to *Matthew*, in a level place according to *Luke*."

"Only $39.95 while they last."

"According to the *Matthew* account, Jesus blessed the 'poor in spirit'… plus those who mourn and would be comforted… plus the meek who would 'inherit the earth', or at least a six-foot-deep plot of dirt, heh, heh… and those who hunger 'and thirst for righteousness' and would be filled. In the account ascribed to Luke, however, Jesus blessed those who were simply poor, not impoverished in 'spirit'… and you who simply hunger now, without mention of thirst for righteousness… and you who weep now, but will later laugh."

"Praise the Lord!" a heavyset Black woman shouted, to further interrupt the flow of his carefully rehearsed opening pitch.

"But wait, there's more. For today only…"

"I put one on layaway, and never regretted it!"

Though tempted to come down from the podium and personally scourge the temple of competitive would-be moneymakers, Roger instead stood silently as ushers took care of the housekeeping chore, then continued:

"The *Luke* account also differs from *Matthew* by its omission of any blessing of the 'merciful'… the 'pure in heart'… the 'peacemakers'. But…"

He paused for oratorical effect.

"Yes, here comes the hitch. In the *Luke* account, deleted 'beplatitudes' scribed in *Matthew* are replaced by 'on the level' warnings spoken by Jesus, to-wit:

"'Woe to you who are rich, for you have already received your comfort.'"

"Amen," someone shouted.

"'Woe to you who are well fed now.'"

Amen! the congregation roared.

"'Woe to you who laugh now, for you will mourn and weep'!"
AMEN!

Though his Church of the Open Hand permitted, indeed encouraged members to put their hands together, no clapping occurred. Nevertheless…

"Of more than forty parables attributed to Jesus in the New Testament, it is telling that the short, pithy story of the loaves and fishes—viewed by me among other well-educated scholars as a parable—is the only one uncut from all four of the Gospels, to-wit: seemingly twelve loaves and twelve fishes fed a multitude gathered to listen and learn.

"Duh. Though some would call it a supernatural 'miracle', obviously the fat cats present had brought along more than enough fried catfish to further fatten themselves, and only had to be 'encouraged' by the disciples—in the forceful manner of the Reverend Al Sharpton, I suspect—to pony up a fair share of goodies to which others were entitled."

Clap. Clap. Clap…

"You may wonder who, when, where, and why only certain 'books' —among the many oral and written materials in circulation for centuries following Jesus' death—were canonized. You may be surprised to learn that it was none other than a Roman politician named Constantine, ruler of the Roman Empire—sworn enemy of Christianity and vicious persecutor of members of the early Church—who got the ball rolling at a council of Bishops in Nicaea in the year 325 CE. The ultimate result was official acceptance of twenty-seven 'books as holy writ'… unification of the Church…and, by the way, adoption of Christianity as the Empire's state religion."

Ohhh…

"Why? Why would the Empire seemingly surrender to a subversive threat to its continued power? Well, as the old saying goes: better to have your opponents inside your tent, urinating outward, heh, heh. In other words, the Empire cleverly co-opted Christianity, corrupted both its leaders and followers, and made the Church an instrument of government oppression."

Ohhhhh…

"But that was not the end of it," Roger declared, "not by a long shot. After more than a thousand years of continued resistance, true Christians, led by Martin Luther, a humble cleric such as myself…"

"Praise the Lord!"

"… began to roll back exploitation of their religion for right-wing government purposes. In the so-called New World most notably, founders of these United States of America adopted a supreme Law of the Land specifically mandating separation of church and state. But…"

Roger again paused for effect.

"Yeah, here comes that 'but' again," he then said, "heh, heh. We've got Trouble with a capital T and that rhymes with B and that stands for Bible!"

Ohhh…

"Oh yes, despite our success in ousting that right-wing State

Superintendent from office, here in this town a high school teacher in service of the modern-day Empire is attempting to poach from the Church's rightful realm."

Ohhh…

"Contrary to Jesus' admonition that we 'render unto Caesar only things that are Caesar's, and unto God things that are God's', a local academic *apparatchik* of the Empire has brought into a public school classroom a version of the Holy Bible purchased Lord knows where!"

Ohhhhh…

"Order two, and get one free," the returned mercantile pitchman shouted from the rear of the sanctuary. "No unwholesome s-e-x!"

"So yet again, we face the age-old question, to-wit: What would Jesus do?"

♫**Onward, Christian soldiers, marching as to war/ With the cross of Jesus, going on before!…** ♫

As the choir chimed in right on cue, Roger slammed his own version of the New Testament onto the podium, and thumped it with a fist.

♫**At the sign of triumph, Satan's host doth flee/ On, then, Christian soldiers, on to victory!…** ♫

"Matthew tells us that Jesus said, quote: 'I did not come to bring peace on earth, but a sword.' And 'Whoever does not take up their cross and follow me is not worthy.'"

♫**Like a mighty army, moves the church of God/ Brothers, we are treading where the saints have trod…** ♫

"Luke tells us that Jesus said, quote: 'I have come to bring fire on the earth, and how I wish it were already burning.' And, quote: 'Do you think I came to bring peace on earth? No, I tell you, but division.'"

♫**We are not divided; all one body we/ One hope and doctrine, one in charity…** ♫

As ushers moved from pew to pew, circulating ceramic bowls shaped as palms-up hands, Roger explained that in the name of the Church of the Open Hand, he had taken legal action to stop the Empire's renewed power grab in public schools.

♫**Onward then, ye people, join our happy throng…** ♫

Tomorrow a public trial of an non-frocked usurper of Jesus' message would take place. Truth and justice would prevail…

♫**Blend with ours your voices in the triumph song…** ♫

… but their victory would no doubt be appealed to a higher court of the Empire, and prolonged judicial process would be costly.

♫**Onward Christian soldiers, marching as to war/ With the cross of Jesus going on before…** ♫

Members of the het-up congregation were now on their feet… enthusiastically singing the second selected hymn along with the choir… eager to hear his upcoming sermon, but…

Down a center aisle, Roger noticed a somehow "different looking" youngish woman standing in the rear of the sanctuary:

A strawberry-blonde, obviously not a member of the Black or Hispanic communities…

Wearing a faded orange tee-shirt, but not a homeless person, he sensed…

Also wearing faded jeans, but not a "butchy" member of the LGBTQ community, he surmised…

And she appeared to be scribbling in a notebook.

Hmmm.

As a preacher who had delivered countless "pitches" for progressive Christian causes to thousands, Roger had a feeling the young strawberry-blonde woman was not inclined to "buy".

CHAPTER 5

Following a brief break for lunch with Wynona Sue and Orville McCarthy at iHOP, Henrietta drove her Checker into the south part of town, thinking about what Reverend Roger Robinson had said from a podium at the Church of the Open Hand.

Following a not so brief "preamble"—and circulation of "open hands" to collect funds for his lawsuit against Mr. Bradley—the wordy preacher had gone on to deliver an even longer-winded smarty-pants lecture about "what Jesus would do" that sounded a lot like the weekly cable news commentary of Ms. Rachel Maddow on MSNOW.

Specifically, he contended that true accounts of Jesus' life and teachings had been "adulterated" by early Christian authorities in a attempt to gloss over demands for political revolution and appease the oppressive "Empire" now being run by Republicans.

Advising the congregation to not count on the Bible's accounts of miracles and "saccharin sayings" attributed to Jesus, the smuggish sumbitch suing Mr. Bradley for having a Bible in a high school classroom thumped his own copy of the New Testament part and thundered that the only reliable accounts in it were those in which Jesus told disciples that it was almost impossible for rich people to get into heaven… that everyone should sell their possessions and give proceeds to the poor…. that anyone who gave nothing for hungry people to eat, nothing for thirsty people to drink, no clothes for others to wear, no free healthcare to others…and turned away strangers from Mexico… were cursed into an eternal fire prepared for the devil.

The facts of the matter, he claimed, were that what Jesus

actually did was raise hell about a corrupt political system and get hisself crucified for "sedition".

Also claiming that a Biblical chapter titled *Revelations* was too profound to be understood by anyone except PhD scholars such as his own self, the bookish blowhard had explained that the last chapter of the New Testament contained coded truth that got slipped past Empire and Church big shots, including truth that a city named Babylon—secretly meaning Rome—was headquarters for an Empire ruled over by a Beast—secretly meaning an Emperor invested with power of a dragon—meaning none other than Satan… and that the Empire was still up-and-running at headquarters in Washington, D.C. and state capital outposts under the thumb of a current tyrannical Beast.

Arrived at the little ol' house where Mr. Bradley lived, Henrietta got out of the Checker and knocked on the front door. Let inside and offered a seat in a cozy living room, she told the client about the research and investigation into matters bearing on tomorrow's court trial that she had so far conducted.

"Oh yes, little redheaded Roger Robinson," said the old school teacher with a sigh. "Roger was not a good student, as I recall, but unusually opinionated and memorably mouthy. Not popular with his peers, and a perennial losing candidate for Student Council. I was surprised to hear he became a preacher instead of a politician, but…

"From what I hear, Roger Robinson—like some people these days seem to be more Democrat and Republican than American—is more of a political 'Churchman' than religious Christian. More of a 'union organizer' than shepherd, who… Well, he strikes me as not unlike the overly zealous sheepdog in *Far From the Madding Crowd* that drove its master's flock over a cliff."

As for his own understanding of the Bible, Mr. Bradley said that, "perhaps trite but true", he was "spiritual but not officially religious" in the way of being a current churchgoer. "Even as a lad, made to attend Sunday school and church sermons, I had an intuitive sense that Jesus was a 'mystic'. And that his message was primarily concerned not with social behavior so much as, well, as another trite but in my view true saying goes: I felt that his Word was that we are not humans having occasional spiritual experiences, but essentially spiritual beings having a passing human experience.

"According to the *Book of John*, when grilled by Pontius Pilate about whether he was a political figure—would-be King of the Jews—Jesus answered that his kingdom was not of this world, and that if his kingdom was of this world, his followers would have taken up arms. So to me, when Jesus tells us to, say, give away our possessions, hisprimary concern is not for the recipients of charity but with the soul of the giver. As when he also says it's especially hard for a rich man to get into heaven, I believe he means that worldliness is a distraction to our spiritual awareness.

"Others—such as Roger Robinson, it seems—see Christian religion as mainly involving a collective endeavor of church congregations—sort of like the progressive wing of the Democrat party—to promote social, political and economic justice here and now on earth. To them, Jesus' death and resurrection is not enough—compared to, say—raising hell about enforcement of immigration laws—to avoid eternal damnation," the old school teacher said. "Not the kind of pastoring likely to be of much comfort to someone on a death bed, but to each his own, I say.

"Our differences are just a minor politicized footnote to the eternal debate—started by disagreement between the Apostles Paul and James—about whether the ticket into 'heaven' is earned by faith or worldly deeds."

As for his understanding of the Constitutional rule he had allegedly broke, the Defendant in tomorrow's court trial correctly said that the United States Constitution did not actually contain the commonly misunderstood term "separation of church and state", coined—he added—by Thomas Jefferson as shorthand for the rule that government was not allowed to "make a law respecting an establishment of religion, or prohibiting the free exercise thereof."

"What Jefferson said in full—and what I believe—is that

each person's religious faith is each person's garden in the wilderness of the world. For me, that 'garden' is for solitary meditation, spiritually communing with an Almighty, and with my late wife, Kathryn, who remains the love of my life."

Though touched by the sentiment matching her own feelings about Gaylord Goodheart, Henrietta asked the only question that legally mattered.

Old Mr. Bradley answered that while he did in fact keep a copy of his New Testament handy in the classroom, and occasionally referred to its existence and content in terms of their impact on the history and culture of western civilization, he had never intentionally taught any religious point of view to high school students.

Semi-satisfied, Henrietta took her leave and headed back to the Trudgeon Street house, dreading that she would have to buy a Bible from Wynona Sue's new fiancé and at least skim it during likely all-night preparation for tomorrow's trial.

CHAPTER 6

"Good morning, Judge," said T-P's usually observant clerk, though in fact it should have been plain from his demeanor that it was a bad "morning after" a misspent Sunday of miscommuning with the Almighty.

Damnit, after being jolted out of "the zone" by masked anarchists on the seventh green, a slightly errant shot on the eighteenth hole—made more errant by a sudden gust of wind—had resulted in his golf ball striking the trunk of a tree… then bouncing off a large rock…into the one-and-only fairway sand trap on the entire golf course… from where he had hit the ball into a water hazard guarding the green… forcing him—even after granting himself a thirty-foot, one-putt "Gimme"—to card a total score of 101!

And now inside his chambers, damnit, the printed docket lying on his desk indicated that case of *Church of the Open Hand LLC et al vs. Bradley* had not been sensibly settled between parties to the lawsuit, and was scheduled for trial this morning. To make matters even worse…

"Neither Plaintiff nor Defendant wants a jury to decide issues of fact," his clerk confirmed, with a grin on her chubby face. "So a trial will give us an opportunity to shine in the public eye."

T-P didn't feel up to shining. He wanted to be on the country club practice range, out of the public eye, but…

"In your absence on Friday, I agreed that WOKC-TV in Oklahoma City can set up a camera in court and…"

"Televise the trial? Damnit, you should have checked with me first."

"You were on the golf course practice range, and left strict orders not to be disturbed. And besides, Judge Dwight, we're up for re-election."

Exactly! He was up for re-election, and the Church of the Open Hand case against a local high school teacher would require him to make a no doubt controversial decision without guidance of a clear dictate from higher authority. In short, he was out of his "comfort zone" and would be required to decide matters of fact and law on his own.

The Oklahoma Supreme Court seemed to have declared that a now former Oklahoma Education Department Secretary's proposed purchase of Bibles for public school classrooms had violated the so-called "separation of church and state clause" of the State and U.S. Constitutions. And though the purchase order had been rescinded by a new Secretary, the higher court's ambiguous decision—nonsensically requiring only that the purchase be put on "pause"—still stood. The issue was muddled. He was in a spotlight, and…

"I was going to surprise you after the election," said his meddlesome clerk, "but given this opportunity for us to shine, well, I've had your new robe upgraded with gold trim, and bought a matching one for myself."

T-P gnashed his teeth. Given the Oklahoma high court's indecisive ruling, the ball was now in the air, so to speak, subject to being blown into God-knew-what sandy, watery, woody and weedy hazards by fierce political crosswinds.

CHAPTER 7

Across the street from the Willis V. Willis storefront law office, Henrietta noticed that a little red car parked at the curb out front of the Okmulgee County Courthouse had a bumper sticker—F' ELON AND THE FELON—pasted across the front where a carmaker's chrome emblem was likely stuck.

Next to the little car, she also noticed that one of those silver so-called CyberTrucks that looked to be straight out of a *Star Wars* movie displayed a bumper sticker saying STRIKE BACK AT THE EMPIRE.

In a courthouse hallway, finding Mr. Bradley to be setting on a bench, slumped forward with his shaggy gray-haired head hung down in his hands, she fibbed that Mr. Willis would likely be coming along shortly... got the client to his feet and marched him into Judge Dwight's courtroom, where... At sight of none other than Morton P. Fisher standing in the courtroom well next to Reverend Roger Robinson, one of those *deja* view feelings came over her.

She had crossed paths with the short, dark-haired American Civil Liberties Union lawyer ten years ago during the trial of Joe Dokes. Back then the feisty ACLU attorney had bragged about previously helping to keep prayer out of public schools, along with tinsel decorations hung in classrooms and fish-shaped pendants hung from necks of female students. Proud as a meringue pie to have fought against references to Bible stories in classrooms, he had claimed the danger that uneducated youngsters might believe some of them was equal to or greater than that of meditation and silent prayer by drivers on public highways.

So she could understand why Morton P. Fisher would be lawyering against Mr. Bradley having a Bible in his classroom and....

"All rise!" a bailiff hollered, as old Judge Dwight parted black curtains behind his elevated bench, wearing what looked to be an also black ballgown decorated with gold braid. "The District Court of Okmulgee County is now in session. The Honorable Judge Timothy Dwight presiding."

Henrietta again got Mr. Bradley to his feet.

"Oyez! Oyez! The Court is now sitting in the matter of *Church of the Open Hand, LLC, et al, vs. Bradley*. All persons having business in the matter are admonished to draw near and give their attention."

"May it please the Court, I am Morton P. Fisher, attorney-at-law representing the Plaintiff," said the ACLU lawyer, sprung up on his toes like a Poodle dog on its hind legs. "As a longtime member of the American Civil Liberties Union, I have a personal interest in this case involving a dire threat to democracy. I am a Jewish person and..."

Looking unpleased, the judge peered over shoulders of those in the well. Henrietta swiveled and saw... Land sakes alive, a television camera was set up in the rear of the courtroom, with a red light turned on. Now she understood that—just like in the Joe Dokes "matter" ten years ago—Morton P. Fisher aimed to make a show trial of the current *Church of the Open Hand et al vs. Bradley* case. Re-swiveled, she then saw that Judge Dwight was looking unpleased at sight of her own appearance at the Defendant's table.

She reminded His Honor who she was...that as a now licensed attorney associated with Mr. Willis V. Willis, Esquire, she was authorized to stand in for her boss... and in fact had already appeared in Court for motions related to mortgage foreclosures and Sheriff's sales of property.

Judge Dwight shifted his eyes left at Morton P. Fisher, back to right at her own self... glanced toward the rear of the courtroom…

"As I was saying, as a Jewish person I have a particular personal interest in how state religion has been used to persecute…"

"For the record, Your Honor," said Henrietta, "according to the dictionary 'religion' is, quote: 'the belief in and worship of a superhuman power' and/or 'a particular system of faith and worship' and/or 'a pursuit or interest to which someone ascribes supreme importance'."

"Noted," said the judge with a look on his face more sour than he'd started off with. But…

"Jewish people are persecuted not only in our ancestral homeland, but right here in the United States," opposing counsel nevertheless continued. "Separation of church and state is the Constitutional bulwark that protects…"

"For the record again, Your Honor: Seeing how Mr. Fisher has brought up the fact of him being Jewish, plus the fact of conditions in Israel—and that ACLU lawyers are prone to cite laws in other civilized countries in support of what the United States Constitution should mean about, say, capital punishment—when it comes to the matter of so-called 'separation of church and state'…"

"Exactly on point!" said her opponent, again practically jumping into air. "In the tyrannical, theocratic countries of the Middle East that relentlessly persecute my people, Israel is the region's only democracy, and sets a good example for…"

Though firmly on the side of Israel against Islamic terrorist groups, Henrietta felt it was her duty to point out that—in her overnight research of the matter of church and state—she had found out that Israel, though a democracy like the United States, described its own self as "both a Jewish and democratic state"… granted automatic citizenship to anyone who professed belief in Judaism… had religious courts with authority over such things as marriage and divorce… laws against doing certain things on the Jewish Sabbath… and exempted religious students from military service.

"Objection, Your Honor!" the pesky ACLU lawyer barked.

"Israel does not have a written constitution."

"Noted," the judge again said. "Now, let's move on and get this two-ball match over with."

"Just one more point, Your Honor," said Henrietta. "Note also that the term 'separation of church and state' is not in the United States Constitution; that the Law of the Land instead says that Congress and States, quote: 'shall make no law respecting an establishment of religion, or prohibiting the free exercise thereof.'"

Though the trial had not even started, Judge Dwight — after looking down at his law clerk with a semi-pleading expression in his eyes — banged his gavel and declared that the Court would be in recess for fifteen minutes.

CHAPTER 8

Seated at a courtroom table with only the back of his head visible to those in attendance and the many others watching on tv, Roger fumed.

Accepting the ACLU lawyer's offer to handle the Church of the Open Hand case *pro bono*—"for good" as opposed to for fee—had been a mistake, he now realized. As the Plaintiff, he himself—not the hired gun—was to have been the star of the show. But Fisher, now returning to the sideline...

Damnit, though their respective progressive organizations were allies in the ongoing fight to make the Empire not great again—for instance, his church and the ACLU had recently joined in a coordinated, mostly peaceful protest in support of the right of poor people to shoplift—the fact of the matter was that in the dog-eat-dog arena of promoting publicity and fund raising for the progressive cause, they were competitors for media and donor support.

"That little strawberry-blonde is a trouble-making Trumpian troller," said the grandstanding attorney in a lame attempt to excuse his poor performance. "And the sleepy redneck judge..."

"You're fired," said Roger. "I myself will handle the case from hereon."

"He who serves as his own lawyer has a fool for a client," the mouthpiece answered, mouthing a worn American Bar Association sales pitch. "Now that the stage is set and I get to the facts of the matter..."

"All rise! The Court is now back in session, the Honorable Judge Timothy Dwight presiding."

Before Roger could get to his feet, Fisher escaped his grasp, stood and bellowed: "Plaintiff calls Ms. Molly Maguire to the stand."

In answer to the lawyer's questions, the young, overweight female proceeded to testify almost as previously rehearsed:

As a former high school student — required by authorities to attend the Defendant's so-called History of Western Civilization class — she had been "dramatized" by the presence of a Bible on the teacher's desk… In particular, she had been "injured" by the story about the mother of Jesus being a virgin, which had made her fearful of sitting on toilet seats… But at the same time, she now *ad libbed*, the story had made her regret "missing out on the fun"…for which she, along with the Church of the Open Hand, deserved to be paid "puny-tive" damages.

Finally, it would now be his turn in the spotlight, but as Roger got to his feet…

"Just a few more questions before you get out of the box, Ms. Maguire," said the strawberry-blonde trouble-maker who had already joined in breaching the Constitutional rule of church-and-state separation by barging into the Open Hand sanctuary yesterday like a jack-booted ICE agent of the Empire. "When you say you were 'dramatized' by…"

"Objection, your Honor!" Fisher, shrieked at the tv camera in the rear of the courtroom. "Counsel is badgering the witness. This is a court of law, not an off-shore C.I.A. interrogation chamber."

As Judge Dwight remained silent, possibly dozing…

"To judge by you your own self obviously being an expectant mama, you must have been not too 'dramatized' to go ahead and have some fun, which leads me to wonder…"

"I'm not knocked up! Not anymore."

Ha, ha, ha, ha, ha…

"The Reverend made me get an abortion."

Ohhhhh… people in the gallery moaned.

"Under a woman's Constitutional right to privacy, Ms. Maguire's body cavity is a temple, protected by separation of church from state and not to be looked into during court proceedings," Fisher pointed out, but...

Ha, ha, ha, ha, ha...

"Did Mr. Bradley his own self ever preach in class that Jesus was birthed by a virgin mother?"

"He didn't have to, duh. Everybody knows it's in the little Bible he kept on his desk, along with a lot of other salty things that the Reverend explained on my Sunday day of rest after me doing good deeds of cleaning his house, washing his clothes and shining his shoes six days a week."

"It sounds to me that you might've been dramatized by what the Reverend said in church 'stead of anything said by Mr. Bradley in the schoolroom. For instance, I my own self heard Reverend Robinson say..."

"Hearsay!" Fisher yelped, again looking toward the camera.

"My turn to speak for myself!" Roger shouted, rising from his chair.

Ohhhhh...

Loosed from the ACLU lawyer's grip and striding toward the witness stand, inside his head a choir sang ♫*Onward Christian soldiers, marching unto war...* ♫ And after shoving the other witness aside...

"I choose to swear on my own personally edited Bible," he declared, referring to the dog-eared copy of the New testament that he always kept handy, "as courts have ruled is my right under the separation of church and state clause of the Constitution."

"Thanks to the ACLU!" Fisher shouted , again for the benefit of the tv audience.

"Autographed copies of which are available in a set also including the *Communist Manifesto* for only $99.99," Roger announced.

Ohhh...

"Oh yes, Jesus and Marx were both radical progressive revolutionaries."

"And both Jewish, by the way!" Fisher shouted.

"I myself am a Donatist," Roger continued. "During the time that corrupt early-Church leaders renounced the true teachings of Jesus in order curry favor and riches by appeasement of the Empire, the original Donatists — a sect of true believers, based in North Africa and now largely unknown and/or not understood by anyone other than PhD scholars such as myself — fiercely carried on with Jesus' subversive mission."

Though the judge and even some courtroom spectators appeared to be not paying attention, for the benefit of the larger tv audience Roger carried on:

"Initially led by Donatus Magnus, we continue to profess that Christian clergy such as myself must be faultless, and that the Church must be a church of saints, not sinners. Relentlessly repressed by both Empire and Church officials for fomenting civil unrest but supported by common people, we Donatists continue to resist by staging street protests, and taking direct action against so-called private property.

"Not that we are without mercy. Penitents are allowed to beg for the prayers of those entering our church building. They are permitted to kneel inside the sacred sanctuary during my sermons. And are ultimately allowed to stand with the congregation when we sing *Onward Christian Soldiers*.

"Some say our steadfast refusal to surrender to Empire and compromised Church authority contributed to the conquest of North Africa by Islam, to which I say, better a progressive Muslim caliphate than a White Nationalist so-called Christian Empire."

Ohhh...

"Yes, onward Christian soldiers!" Roger shouted, while holding aloft his personalized Bible, "marching on to war with... In my personally edited version of the New Testament, readers will find answers to the question: 'What would Jesus do about Republicans?'"

CHAPTER 9

Henrietta reckoned there would have been no point to interrupting Reverend Robinson's longwinded speech about being a Donatist, not with Judge Dwight nodding off. And besides, Mr. Bradley had took to whispering in her ear after she sat down at the Defendant's table.

The old school teacher didn't want to be part of a windy argument about what the Bible meant to Roger Robinson and others versus what the Jesus story meant to his own self. Again he told that to his own self Jesus' message was personal, and private. He wanted to throw in a towel and take medicine, but...

Again she bucked him up with a quiet pep talk about how miserable he would be if he lost his pension... then looked at her watch.

As the Church of the Open Hand preacher continued to bluster about what else the Bible meant to him, she was reminded of a college boy from Indiana who came through town one Summer when she was in high school... knocking on doors and introducing hisself as "just another ol' Bible salesman"... then launching into a stuttering sales pitch as windy as the one being spouted by Reverend Robinson. But...

Henrietta again looked at her watch.

Ten minutes was long enough for the judge's cat nap, she reckoned. So as the Reverend paused to take a drink of water, she stood up and stomped a foot on the courtroom's wood floor to make as loud a noise as she could. His Honor's head jerked up and...

"Reverend Robinson," she said, "I understand that to you this here trial is about separation of church and state, or as you put it: a continuation of Jesus versus 'Empire'. Is that right?"

"Quite right. Though Theodore Bradley is a rodent of the mouse variety, the instruction of *Song of Solomon* 2:15 applies, to-wit: 'Catch the foxes for us, the little foxes that spoil the vineyards.' Even the smallest breaches in the wall must be vigilantly attended to."

"And you say the idea of a wall between church and state in the Constitution goes back to what is 'writ' in this here Bible," said Henrietta, holding up the copy she had bought from Wynona Sue's new fiancé yesterday. "Specifically, you say that the idea sprang from the *Matthew* chapter in which Jesus says, to-wit: 'Render therefore unto Caesar the things that are Caesar's; and unto God the things that are God's.' Is that right?"

"There's much more to the 'idea' than that, but in simple terms for the uneducated, heh, heh, yes: 'Caesar' translates to 'Empire' and 'God' translates to 'Church'."

"And with regard to the 'more to it' part suggested by the words 'therefore' and 'things', ain't it true that what Jesus said was in answer to someone asking if monetary tribute should be paid to 'Caesar'?"

"*Matthew* is clear that we cannot serve two masters!" the holder of a PhD—in Public Relations, according to his *Wikipedia* page—shouted. Launching into what would no doubt have been a wordy explanation that the question—the one put to Jesus—was a trick…

"Is the cover of that Bible real leopardskin?" said Judge Dwight. "It would match my wife's Sunday leotards. Where did you…?"

"Only $39.95," Henrietta heard the Bible salesman, Orville McCarthy, holler from the gallery.

"And Orville offers matching Mister-and-Missus deals for couples to look at while in bed!" Wynona Sue added.

"What I was getting at, Reverend," Henrietta continued, "is that your Church of the Open Hand don't pay 'tribute' to the government in the form of taxes on revenue and real estate. But you're not het-up about that cozy relationship between church and state, are you, even though taxes go toward funding of the progressive government programs you mainly preach about."

"Greedy corporations and rich people hire high-priced lawyers to get out of paying fair taxes that mainly go to funding the Empire's oppression of people here and around the world! That's corrupt politics. Exemption of my church from taxes…"

"And according to my Googling the matter, that advice Jesus gave about paying taxes was the one-and-only time he ever mentioned a 'Caesar' or anything else having to do with the so-called 'Empire' you ranted against in yesterday's sermon."

"Preachers and Biblical scholars such as myself—dating back to those who first put scripture into writing—are trained to read between spoken lines and interpret what Jesus meant to say. It's called theology, without which common people would not understand Bibles."

"On the other hand, Jesus had plenty to plainly say against know-it-all preachers," Henrietta pointed out. "Seven times in a single Bible chapter Jesus said, 'Woe to you, teachers of the law of the Pharisees, you hypocrites!' for centering attention on your own selves, preaching and practicing religion wrong, and making it harder for people to get into a kingdom of God."

Ohhh…

"I will not stoop to respond to uneducated *ad hominem* attacks from such as you," said the Reverend. "For the benefit of others who have eyes to see and ears to hear, suffice it to say that scholars such as myself understand that Jesus' authorization of payment of tribute to Caesar was a foxy stalling tactic to temporarily avoid a two-front war. In addition to being threatened by the Empire, he was also confronted by Jewish religious authorities. And, as you may have heard but do not understand, Jesus went on to take direct revolutionary action by ridding the Temple of capitalist money-changers and merchants!"

Ohhh…

"Speaking of money changing hands and merchandising in temples, what about sales of Bibles with your picture on the covers that are displayed for sale in the lobby of the Church of the Open Hand, along with your books, bumper stickers, and mugs?"

"The Bible tells us to spread the Word, and that God empowers us to receive our rewards and rejoice in our labor."

"Uh huh, but what about other not so religious words spread in temples, such as the hour-long sermon you your own self delivered from the pulpit of the Church of the Open Hand yesterday that was almost word-for-word a political speech such as could've been made by Senator Bernie Sanders on a campaign trail?"

"Senator Sanders is a secular Jew, and takes his speeches from ACLU publications," Morton P. Fisher declared.

"Senator Sanders is a modern-day prophet," said the Reverend, "not unlike the John who later had an inspired dream and in *Revelations* relayed God's message to the congregation in Sardis, to-wit: 'Wake up, for if you do not wake up, I will come like a thief, and you will not know at what hour I come against you.' Oh yes, revolutionary 'wokism' comes straight from the Bible."

Ohhh...

"But even though the Internal Revenue Service has a rule that, for churches to get out of paying taxes, preachers such as your own self are not allowed to spout about politics, what about your praise from a pulpit for a Mr. Che Guevara, who I also Googled and found to have been a blood-thirsty... ?"

"Saint Che was a modern-day 'thirteenth disciple', far more deserving than the mealy-mouth 'Apostle Paul' to take the place of Judas. As put in the Gospel of Jesus' own brother, James—to-wit: 'What good is it if someone has faith but has no deeds?'—the martyred Che told us, to-wit: 'Words without deeds are worthless.'"

In a statement with a lawyerly question mark at the end, Henrietta opined that Reverend Robinson his own self regularly breached the wall between church land state on a one-way street that allowed "faultless saints" such as his own self to spout about politics like Muslim terrorists firing rockets from sacred mosques, while not allowing poor old Mr. Bradley to even have a Bible in his classroom.

"Aha! You admit Bradley has been 'firing back' at the church like an Israeli storm trooper!" the Reverend bellowed.

Ohhh...

"The Palestinian terrorists started it," Morton P. Fisher hollered, "then hid in heavily armed mosques and hospitals in an attempt to get world sympathy for separation of church and state!"

Reverend Robinson then answered her question by saying that neither the Bible nor the Constitution were "town ordinances that laid out streets". To the contrary, he said, when Jesus spoke of "the Way" and commanded people to follow him, he meant for true believers to go "off-road", maneuver around the "wall", and wage "guerrilla warfare" to destroy the Empire.

Ohhh...

"Well now, we don't go that far," the ACLU lawyer quibbled. "But matters of public interest have always been legitimate subjects of, uh, discourse in churches and synagogues. And you yourself, Counselette, introduced dictionary evidence in this very trial that one of the definitions of 'religion' is pursuit of an interest to which one ascribes supreme importance."

"Heh, heh, hoisted on your own petard," said Robinson, standing up to take his leave from the witness box. "I daresay, Miss whomever you are, that you would be better suited for work as a magistrate for the State. Openly operating as an agent of the Empire, you might have some success at prosecuting defenseless, young Black, handicapped members of the LBGQT community for shoplifting a few loaves of bread. But when debating weightier matters with scholars such as myself..."

For all his bold jabber about about being a "subversive revolutionary" along the lines of Che Guevera, Henrietta had a notion that the Reverend was just a partisan political hack more along the lines of that New York Senator who was all the time shaking a fist on tv and threatening 'resistance' to Republicans. With her dander up, she stated that it looked to her that he his own self was trying to "establish a state religion" from the pulpit of his church…

"Nonsense. It just so happens that only the Democrat Party…"

… then asked the witness about the part of his sermon yesterday in which he told the Church of the Open Hand congregation that "what Jesus would do" was "resist the Beast currently in charge ot the Empire," and not vote for the re-election of Judge Dwight unless and until he, the saintly scholar, told them to.

Ohhh…

The Reverend stopped in his tracks, gave her a look that could have iced-down a keg of beer, and said: "Woe unto judges who issue unrighteous decrees, and to the magistrates who argue in favor of them."

Though she had planned and expected that her loaded question would have a powerful effect on the judge, Henrietta looked up and saw… Dang it, His Honor looked to have fell sound asleep.

CHAPTER 10

Remember the Sabbath, and keep it holy...

T-P dreamed he was standing in the grassy fairway of the country club's eighteenth hole on a Sunday...communing with Nature in the open-air Church of Pantheism... needing only to make an easy shot to the final green... where invocation of the Two-Putt Rule would entitle him to card a 5... and result in a score of ninety-nine for the round. But...

Damnit, instead of a nine-iron, he had in hand... a gavel?

Woe unto judges who issue unrighteous decrees. If you are not woke, you won't know what hit you...

"Judge, wake up," he heard his clerk hiss.

T-P's eyes popped open.

"The Defendant has filed a denial of the Plaintiff's allegations in *Church of the Open Hand, et al vs. Bradley* and Plaintiff has presented its evidence. Time for us to rise and shine."

During the earlier recess his assistant had briefed him on the issues of law raised by the lawsuit at hand, to-wit: The U.S. Supreme Court had handed down multiple decisions allowing Bibles in public school classrooms — provided that the books were not used for "devotional" instruction — but Constitutional water had been muddied by the Oklahoma Supreme Court decision to put a temporary block on purchase of Bibles for schools by the former Secretary of Education. Local school boards, teachers, and some parents continued to be het-up about...

"Judge Dwight sits with one buttock on the bench of Pontius Pilate and one buttock on the Bible upon which he swore an oath to serve the cause of justice," the Plaintiff was saying to the television camera. "Woe to him if he makes the wrong decision in this case."

Hmmm.

T-P shifted his weight but… Contrary to being finished with presentation of his case, the Plaintiff turned to face the bench and—now looking and sounding a lot like the leader of the band of hooligans who had accosted him on the golf course yesterday—thundered:

"On behalf of the Plaintiffs in this matter, including myself, I call to the stand the Defendant, Theodore 'Baggy Pants' Bradley."

As opposing lawyers proceeded to engage in tedious legal argle-bargle about the Defendant's right not to possibly incriminate himself, T-P raised his gavel, intending to wash his hands of the entire case, but…

"I'll swear on my own copy of the New Testament," said the old school teacher, taking the stand, then reciting the standard oath to tell the truth.

"Ah, we meet again," said the Plaintiff to the Defendant. "Remember me, Bradley? I am the student you expelled for…"

"For theft, as I recall. Yes, I well remember you, Mister Robinson."

"I was following Robin Hood's example by robbin' from the rich. And by the way, it's Doctor Robinson. No thanks to your pathetic pedagoguing, I went on to attend a Yale Divinity School seminar, and have since been awarded a PhD."

"'Robbin' from the Save the Children donations box, as I further recall."

"Not just poor children were in need, Bradley, but nice try at dodging your comeuppance. As an ordained minister and Biblical scholar, charged with protecting religion from appropriation by the Empire, I put to you this question: Have you or have you not made a practice of bringing that Bible of yours into a public school classroom? Yes or no?"

T-P again shifted his weight and crossed his fingers, hoping for an admission by Defendant that would bring the trial to an end without matters of disputed fact to be…

"The answer is yes, I kept my New testament on hand…"

Phew.

"… but only for occasional references in connection with the role of the book's existence and content in the history of western civilization. To do otherwise would be like trying to explain the seventy-year history of the Soviet Union—not to mention current China—without reference to the *Communist Manifesto* by Karl Marx."

Damnit, now he would have to decide…

"Ha! What 'role' of the Bible did you 'reference' that is not Constitutionally reserved for the realm of religion and correctly taught only in church by Biblical scholars such as myself?"

"Actually, while it's true that state and church ruled their respective European 'realms' somewhat separately for centuries," said the high school teacher, "the facts are that translation of the Bible from Greek and Latin understood only by clerics went hand-in-hand with invention of the printing press to spread the Reformation that—along with popular literacy—fundamentally altered virtually every aspect of western civilization."

"Including establishment of the British state religion created by Henry VIII and later brought to these shores," the ACLU lawyer howled. "It took a revolutionary war and intense progressive lawyering to get rid of it. And a Constitution to protect…"

"The revolutionary war rages on!" the combative preacher raged. "While oppressing the people and enriching itself, the Empire is a pusher of what Marx correctly called the opiate of the masses, a concoction of inane moralisms and quaint sayings about… For instance, <u>Mister</u> Bradley, did you not traumatize your student, Molly Maguire, by making 'occasional references' to the Bible's claim of Jesus' virgin birth?"

"No, never. Nor did I ever…"

"How about the account of the resurrection of Jesus? How could you not 'make reference' to the the otherwise mostly good book's' central mistaken idea—fostered by the duplicitous Apostle Paul—that people should tolerate a miserable earthy existence in hope of being gifted with social justice in an afterlife?"

T-P's eyelids again began to droop.

"Everything about the virgin birth and resurrection of Jesus has been stripped from my Bible," said the witness, holding up the copy of the Good Book he'd sworn upon.

Ohhhhh courtroom spectators gasped.

"Stripped from the Bible you employed in the classroom?" said the Plaintiff.

Ohhhhh…

"That's tampering with evidence, Your Honor!" the annoying ACLU lawyer shouted. "Throw the book at this… this stripper!"

Ohhhhh…

Two-Putt again shifted his weight…again peered down at his clerk for guidance… but got from her in return only an indecipherable throat-cutting signal.

CHAPTER 11

In the glare of Judge Dwight's wide-open stink-eye, Henrietta squirmed in her chair like sinful "streetwalkers" were said to do in church.

She had told Mr. Bradley it would be okay for him to take his own Bible onto the stand for making an oath to truthfully testify, not knowing he had tampered with what was evidence of Reverend Robinson's accusation that he'd made unallowed references to the book in his classroom. What might have turned out to be a judgement against the retired teacher requiring payment of affordable damages had turned into threatened worse trouble for both him and her own self. And now…

Sure enough, the Plaintiff pounced at the Defendant with a gotcha look in his eye and…

"I daresay scripture stripped from that Bible of yours are Jesus' calls for revolution and overthrow of the Empire," Reverend Robinson dared say. "I daresay that—while retaining the off-message passages later added by corrupted scribes and now used by White Nationalists to support fascist notions of 'moral absolutes', 'traditional values', 'personal responsibility' etcetera—you stripped from the true Gospels the thrust of Jesus' marching orders," said the preacher, before turning around to face the tv camera and shouting, "to-wit:

"Just as Karl Marx told us to 'lose' the chains of capitalism—and declared, 'From each according to his abilities and to each according to his needs'—Jesus commands us to rid ourselves of possessions and give to the poor, for 'from each to whom much is given, much is expected.'"

Ohhh… the gallery audience again ohhhed.

"Just as President Biden reminded us that his own esteemed family were immigrants—and put out a welcome mat for people from around the world to cross the so-called Mexican border—the Bible tells us that so too were Jesus and his family…not Mexicans, but immigrants. And as even the usually wishy-washy Apostle Paul wrote in his epistle to the Church in Jerusalem: 'Some people have shown hospitality to angels without knowing it.'"

Ohhh…

"Just as brave leaders of the Black Lives Matter movement continue to fight for elimination of the racist Goldilocks notion of the Papa Bear-Mama Bear-Little Bear 'nuclear family', Jesus tells us he 'came to turn sons against fathers, daughters against mothers', and that you are to follow educated Church leaders who speak the word of God."

Ohhh…

"In short, Jesus was a Marxist revolutionary who today would urge us to burn down for-profit business establishments and fight for redistribution of wealth…"

Ohhh…

"…an anti-nationalist, who would today be fighting alongside Mexicans and Palestinians to erase artificial borders signifying American and Israeli occupation of their ancestral lands…"

Ohhh…

"…and an Antifa protestor who would be the first to throw a Molotov cocktail to spark anarchy and collapse of the Empire!"

Ohhh…

"Of course there are always among us those who cherry-pick words attributed to Jesus…"

Ohhh…

"… defile his rightful messenger…"

Ohhh…

"… and attempt to usurp the role of ordained ministers such as myself."

Ohhh…

Henrietta looked over her shoulder, half expecting to see ushers handing out bowls in the shape of open hands.

"Let's have a look at what you chose <u>not</u> to strip from your Bible," said the Biblical scholar, holding his own open hand out to the witness. "Not the wimpy 'sayings', I daresay."

"As a matter of fact, no; Jesus' sayings—such as 'Turn the other cheek'—are intact, along with…"

Uh oh, at church yesterday Henrietta had heard Reverend Robinson declare, almost just like he said about Judge Dwight's buttocks…

"Ha! What Jesus said was that if one were to be slapped on the <u>right</u> cheek," he now repeated, "one was to turn his left cheek to his assailant. For a Roman would have struck a Christian with a backhanded slap delivered by his right hand. For a Jesus follower to turn his cheek and stand as an equal would have been an act of revolutionary defiance."

Ohhhhh…

"The correct meaning of words spoken by Jesus depends on context understood only by scholars such as myself. Agents of the Empire such as Bradley foster ignorance of all-important context and…"

Swiveled from facing the tv cameras to again face the witness, "I daresay you did not you strip from your so-called Bible the Apostle Paul's noxious notion that faith—not deeds—is required of Jesus' followers."

Henrietta her own self had a notion that what the matter at hand came down to was that Mr. Bradley was a square peg, so to speak, and Reverend Robinson a round one, both stuck in misfitting holes. If there was to be separation of church and state as required by the U.S. Constitution, they ought to trade places to her way of thinking…with the so-called Reverend teaching about history and politics in a classroom, and the old school teacher leading silent prayer from a pulpit. But her client was wrongly stuck and…

"Wrong again, Roger: I myself never did any stripping," he now claimed. "It was Thomas Jefferson who 'tampered' with this

Bible."

Ohhh…

Thomas Jefferson?

"The so-called Jefferson Bible?!" said the Church of the Open Hand preacher, eyeing the cover of the thin book handed over to him with the gotcha look turned to one of confused irritation. "You spitefully purchased and brought to a classroom this…this edited version of the New Testament instead of spending a few dollars more for…?"

"Thomas Jefferson was a slave owner and sexual abuser of Black women!" Morton P. Fisher shrieked.

Ohhhhh…

"Leave this to me, Counselor!" Roger Robinson barked at the ACLU attorney, as he thumbed through the "tampered" evidence; then raised his red-haired head and announced: "Jefferson was a turncoat and walked in the shoes of Judas!"

Ohhhhh…

"Oh yes, in private letters the once radical revolutionary relished the slaughter of aristocrats and *bourgeoisie* during the so-called 'Reign of Terror' phase of the French Revolution. Openly, Jefferson wrote, quote: 'The tree of liberty must be refreshed from time to time with the blood of patriots and tyrants. It is its natural manure.'"

Ohhhhh…

"But when it counted, by actions speaking louder than words, Jefferson—no less despicably than what Judas did for thirty pieces of silver—sold-out to the Empire and became it's Beast!"

Ohhhhh…

"Only in repentant dotage did he finally cut-and-paste to produce an accurate Bible relatively free of state-sponsored superstitions that mute Jesus' call for revolution!"

Ohhh.

Henrietta stood, stomped a foot and declared that it looked to her own self that Reverend Robinson had admitted that Mr. Bradley's stripped-down copy of the Bible did not meet the main definitions of "religion" and…"

"Ha!" Morton P. Fisher snorted. "You yourself, 'Counselor', have already effectively stipulated that the Constitution's ban on establishment of 'religion' could be read to apply to, quote: 'pursuit of interest in matters of supreme importance'," the ACLU lawyer repeated.

Ohhh.

"Only to show that the objection to Mr. Bradley having a Bible in class could be 'read' as applying to references to almost any other dang book about important history and politics that ought to be interesting to teenagers."

Ohhhhh...

Judge Dwight, known to be an extra-proud of making it through one-semester as a student at the University of Virginia—where about everyone was said to downright worship memory of its founder, Thomas Jefferson—directed a fish-eye at the Reverend. But the preacher had again turned his back to the judge to again look at the tv camera.

"Nothing Thomas Jefferson ever did, said, wrote or cut-and-pasted is fit to be allowed on public school premises!" Morton P. Fisher hollered.

Bang!

"The court will not tolerate blasphemy in its presence," Judge Dwight declared after banging his gavel. "Church of the Open Hand *et al* are hereby ordered to pay court costs, plus Defendant's legal fees and expenses. Court adjourned."

Ohhhhh...

All of which just went to show—to Henrietta's way of thinking—that when it came to matters of politics and religion, sure enough, words took from—or left in—both the Bible and United States Constitution could be made to dance like angels—or devils—on the tip of a tongue or pen.

THE
END

HUFFING & PUFFING

THE BIG BAD WOLF
"Little pig, little pig, let me come in."
"Not by the hair of my chinny-chin-chin."
The big bad wolf huffed, and he puffed…

English Fairy Tale

SIMON PLASTER

CHAPTER 1

♫So I called up to the Captain/ "Please bring me my wine"/ He said, "We haven't had that spirit/ since 1969"…♫

Henrietta sat at her desk in the lobby of the Okmulgee, Oklahoma storefront law office of Willis "V-for-Versus" Willis, reading an online article that had brought to mind the famous old song called *Hotel California.*

Willis, a member of the bar for almost forty years, was still locally famous as a litigator in the so-called "adversarial system" that pitted Somebody vs. Somebody to supposedly bring out truth in matters of disagreement. He was reputed to have at least once appeared in court as attorney for both plaintiff and defendant in the same contentious case. But…

Involvement in constant fussing and fighting — especially in divorce cases — looked to have finally took its toll on her boss, who was nowadays more active at the nearby 24/7 Happy Hours Hangout located catty-corner from the Okmulgee County Courthouse.

♫Mirrors on the ceiling/ Pink champagne on ice/ She said, "We're all just prisoners here, of our own device…♫

According to the online article on her computer screen, addiction was a "neuropsychological disorder characterized by a persistent and intense urge to ingest a substance or engage in behavior that produces natural reward." The common denominator for addictions to even shopping, gambling, pornography, sex, news, social media, video games, and risky activity was brain production of something coincidentally called "dopamine" that made people feel temporarily good about things.

But resulted afterward in negative consequences such as irritability and anger, fearful paranoid anxiety, chronic engagement in conflicts, and—in the case of Willis' inclination to overindulge in the company of "Jim Barleycorn"—changes in personality and attitude, lack of motivation, and—dang it—decreased workplace attendance and performance.

♫ *"Relax," said the night man/ "We are programmed to receive/ You can check out anytime you like/ But you can never leave"*... ♫

"Andrew Jackson needs a pettifogger!" a female voice exclaimed.

Henrietta looked up from the laptop screen and saw that a raggedy-dressed elderly gal wearing a red MAGA cap had entered the office lobby…followed by a heavyset, bearded, semi-youngish fella wearing a motorcycle helmet and one of those bulky vests stuffed with sheep fleece.

"Your bench sign says you're a LitiGator, which is just what my boy needs to fight off those riled-up hooligans from Alabama."

Henrietta let slide the walk-in's mistook identification of her own self as the advertised reptile, told the agitated mama and her "boy" to take seats across from her, and started jotting on a pad of paper.

Ms. Irene Reilly said she had drove her son downtown and, while he tended to an errand, had ducked into the 24/7 Happy Hours Hangout for refreshment.

Andrew Jackson Reilly looked up from his phone—announced that the country was on a brink of civil war—and said he had been at the Mithril Adventures store across the street, playing *The Wolf Among Us* video game while waiting for his PlayStation motherboard to be serviced.

"I was wondering why the Happy Hours regulars were not hanging out at the 24/7 as usual," said the oddish old woman.

"I was playing *Cry Wolf,* the first season's final episode of the Telltale game," said the odder son, before returning attention to his phone.

"When the barroom door opened, I heard racket…"

"Someone with bad rhythm was beating a drum."

"Down the street, right out there in front of the courthouse…"

"Civil disorder was in progress."

"The Happy Hours crowd was there, watching the fracas. Someone threw a beer bottle and…"

"I don't imbibe fermented hops, which are a major cause of potentially explosive flatulence."

"An aggravated policeman came along and arrested Andrew Jackson for hateful assault with a battery!"

"You'd think constables had better things to do, what with the town being overrun with lesbians, litterbugs and undocumented Latino lawn mowers."

"I sweet-talked the copper into trusting us to show up for an arrangement in court Monday morning."

"I have a previous engagement that cannot be usurped."

"So here we are, in need of a fixer."

"Corrupt judges are more than happy to arrange release of Venezuelan gangbangers."

Henrietta told that she would make sure Andrew Jackson had legal representation at Monday's "arrangement" in old Judge Dwight's courtroom, and that as for fees…

"I put another mortgage on the house and sent Andrew Jackson off to an institution, but he came back."

"I studied the scribblings of the Irish thinker, Jonathan Swift, and mastered those of the French Renaissance philosopher, Michel de Montaigne."

"Andrew Jackson is an intellectual, which means a know-it-all, but can't or won't hold a steady job."

"I often quote couplets of Swift and Montaigne insights to—like Montaigne himself—better express my own thoughts."

"I had to quit working at the Goodwill Store on account of having the arthritis in my hips, and my disability payments hardly cover…"

"Mother denies it, but rickety hips in old women are usually a result of frenzied be-bop dancing in their younger days."

"Andrew Jackson helps around the house, but mainly just wastes time in the basement, playing with hisself."

"Sometimes I commune with other Wolfies on the Onanon platform."

"He won't leave the house to go look for a job."

"I have to keep up with breaking news," the new client said, before again looking at his phone. "The country is beset with gibers, censurers, attorneys, bawds, buffoons, politicians, wits, splenetics, tedious talkers, controvertists, as well as leaders and followers of party and faction."

"If my boy gets thrown into jail, he'll have another reason not to find gainful employment," Ms. Reilly wailed.

"As noted by Swift, how vain it is for a man to attempt to do himself honor among a confederacy of those who are out of all degree of equality or comparison with him."

Henrietta told the Reillys that fees for services could be worked out and began to think about legal grounds for defending Andrew Jackson at his arraignment for assault and battery.

Hmmm.

Diminished capacity to intend what he did at the fracas with hooligans came to mind. Jumpy as spit on a skillet while repeatedly looking at his phone, the oddster sure enough looked to be addicted to some kind of unhealthy behavior affecting his brain.

CHAPTER 2

Staring at a computer screen, Don Melone contemplated his prospects for returning to elite status as a tv news star. Though now almost sixty, he still had the face, the voice, and—just as importantly—the knack for creating provocative narratives of even commonplace events. In short, he knew how to report news.

Dramatizing conflict of good versus evil was essential—everyone knew that—but more specifically...

As a child, he had been scared shitless by his mother's telling and re-telling of Big Bad Wolf fairytales, especially the one about the wolf's huffing and puffing that destroyed the houses of two little pigs. As a teenager, he had been brought to tearful hysteria by the sudden punchlines of ghost stories, accompanied by a drunken uncle's howling at a full moon. And to this day, gruesome horror movies such as *Silence of the Lambs* continued to arouse sadomasochistc reactions of orgasmic proportion.

As explained by one of his college professors in a long-ago class about Creative Writing, stories *per se* triggered a process called "neural coupling" that resulted from release into the brains of both tellers of tales and listeners a heady cocktail of neurochemicals: cortisol, a stress hormone condusive to capturing attention and establishing an emotional "hook"...oxyfectin that promoted feelings of mutual trust, empathy, and bonding...and dopamine that created a "feel good" mental reaction demanding unending repetition. When coupled with content that evoked fear and anger, a double-dosage of mind-altering chemicals compounded the effect.

In a nutshell, a shrink had later confirmed that he, a

journalist—along with people constantly online and/or watching tv—were doomed to become addicted to ingestion of "news" that confirmed their conditioned sense of belonging to groups of shared intellectual, moral, and political superiority.

Last year on his Onanon.net channel, for instance, he had received a shitload of highly emotional *Likes* for passing on a news story about a reindeer in Alaska that got poisoned, cleverly edited to suggest that "Rudolph" was the victim of a sinister MAGA plot, and scaring the bejeezus out of readers who thought Christmas was in peril. Weak sisters criticized the fear mongering, but...

Hell, Jake Tapper continued to hold a primetime job at CNN, by continuing to tap into rampant Trump derangement syndrome. Rachel Maddow continued to earn big bucks at MSNOW by crying wolf about blood-thirsty hinterland barbarians at the gate. Jesse Waters got the well-paid big chair at Fox News by feeding red meat to red-state rednecks. And Tucker Carlson...

Don seethed with resentment that the disgraced, pretty white-faced pusher of scary right-wing conspiracy theories—fired by even Fox News—had gone on to greater fame and fortune by setting up a paid streaming service on his own TCN platform—while he himself...

Don sighed.

In the wake of his own job loss and exile from the land of elite New York media to his hometown of Oklmulgee, Oklahoma, his Storytime Guy channel had launched with thousands of devoted followers, but...Okay, as a result of debilitating personal issues resulting in loss of fortune and reputation by miscarriage of justice in a lawsuit, his followers had become less devoted and drastically fewer in number, but... He still harbored hope. His return to bigtime journalism surpassing the notoriety undeservedly enjoyed by Tucker Carlson would come, and soon.

In fact, earlier this very day—during his coverage of a colorful but unimportant local event—real news exactly fitting a tried-and-true template had happened right in front of him. And now...With fingers of one hand crossed, Don nudged his computer's mouse with his other hand and settled in to watch for a third time the video he had posted within the past hour:

♫That famous day in history/ the men of the Seventh Cavalry went riding on/ And from the rear a voice was heard/ "Please, Mr. Custer, I don't wanna go"…♫

As background music featuring a dramatic drumbeat set the desired ominous mood, a framing shot of Okmulgee's historic Creek Nation Council House appeared on the screen…that then faded to black. In white letters…

STORYTIME GUY
Rednecks vs. Redskins

"Only months prior to the kindred Sioux tribe's glorious victory in the 1868 Battle of Little Big Horn, the Oklahoma town of Okmulgee—meaning place of 'boiling waters'—was officially established as the capital of the Muscogee Nation of Native Americans commonly known as Creeks," his recorded voice-over announced.

"The Nation is comprised of almost five thousand square miles, extending from the southern suburbs of Tulsa for almost a hundred linear miles southward. Governed by an executive branch led by a Principal Chief, a legislative branch consisting of sixteen elected members representing eight districts, and its own judicial system, the tribe provides its one hundred thousand still oppressed members with an array of vital communal services, including…"

A series of additional framing shots flashed on the screen as the voice-over continued to recite a script lifted from *Wikipedia*, followed by…

♫I had a dream last night about the comin' fight/ Somebody yelled 'Attack!'/ And there I was with an arrow in my back…♫

"Yes, the white man got his comeuppance at the hands of the Sioux, led by Chief Sitting Bull. But today the Creeks are peacefully gathered in their town square in solemn remembrance of the 1813 Fort Mims Massacre back in their ancestral Alabama homeland. Then and there, a brave band of Upper Creek 'Red Sticks' valiantly fought an evil axis of traitorous Lower Creek

'White Sticks' allied with federal ICE agents led by Major General Andrew Jackson in what later proved to be a vain attempt to maintain the tribe's freedom and traditional way of life in the face of overpowering oppression by the white man.

"Defeat of the rebellious Red Sticks by Jackson and cowardly White Sticks in the subsequent 1814 Battle of Horseshoe Bend was followed by conquest of Native American lands throughout the South and displacement of the Creek people, culminating in their tragic 1830s trek to Oklahoma on the infamous Trail of Tears. Despite continued oppression, the Creek Nation now stands proud and strong, but still beset..."

The video shifted to the live action Don had captured with his hand-held phone: a mob surrounding an elderly Native American figure clad in fur and wearing a ceremonial wolf's-head war bonnet.

"Today, water—and blood—boil in Okmulgee, Oklahoma."

♫There's a redskin waitin' out there/ fixin' to take my hair/ A coward I am called/ 'cause I don't wanna end up dead or bald...♫

"The Creek elder shown beating a drum and prayerfully chanting—to judge by the heckling of rednecks surrounding him—is Chief Kaw-Liga. Now watch...

"A beer bottle shatters at the feet of the Chief...who answers with louder drumbeats and chants...joined by cries for justice by outraged fellow Creeks.

"A white thug protected by a motorcycle helmet lunges from the mob of hecklers to menace the venerable elder..."

"Stop him before he commits genocide!' a civilized white woman in the crowd screeched.

Shouting and scuffling broke out and...with a selfie of himself on the screen...

"There you have it," Don vocally observed, "a modern-day attempt by hateful white rednecks to drive Native Americans from their adopted Oklahoma homeland."

"Poor old Kaw-Liga!" the white mob chanted. "Poor old..."

Even better, with his phone returned to focusing on the swarm of rednecks continuing to viciously mock the venerable

Creek Chief…

"A uniformed policeman seizes the white hooligan…later identified as <u>Andrew</u> <u>Jackson</u> Reilly!" Don announced. "And…"

Ping!

Ping!

Ping!

Don looked at his phone and…Geronimo! His Onanon channel was being flooded with posts!

Let's hope Chief Kaw-Liga is not sexually active, 'cause as Professor Churchill pointed out many moons ago, there's more than one way to commit genocide against Native Americans, and sex with white people is the worst.

Right on, Sister. Professor Ward Churchill is part Creek Indian, and knows what he was talking about. I had the high honor of studying under the wise man at the University of Colorado in 2005, and—after drinking alcohol that white devils had introduced to subdue previously undrugged Native Americans—I got the pox from the blanket the Feds gave him.

In one of his books—it might have been INDIANS ARE US?—Churchill said he was 52.8 pounds Indian—about 35 pounds Creek and the remainder Cherokee—88.0 pounds Teutonian, 43.5 pounds some sort of English, and the rest undetermined.

His point was that so-called blood quantum laws for determining Native Americanhood by degrees of blood treats Native Americans like dogs and horses, and that inter-ethnic sex would ultimately define them out of existence.

Other tactics of cultural genocide were to force so-called assimilation with white colonist ways at Indian boarding schools, and assigning Native American mascots to shitty sports teams!

Redskins is not a slur. To the contrary, as Don mentioned at the end, the term relates to the bloody foreskins that Native American braves bit off the dicks of white men, and hung in their wig-wams as trophies.

As the comments and thumbs-up continued like a mostly peaceful Black Lives Matter street demonstration, Don leaned back in his chair with satisfaction.

Keep beating that war drum, Chief Kaw-Liga! We've got your back.

Let's take more Montezuma's revenge on old white men!

Death to the redneck, <u>Andrew Jackson</u> Reilly!

Make him burn in hell with George A. Custer!

Let's take Trump's blondish combed-over scalp!

Bite-off Trump's whole dick, Don! And his balls!

Mr. Melone, call me ASAP! Peg Patterson at OKC-TV in Oklahoma City.

Don sat upright with a jerk.

Peg Patterson was the longtime host of a regular WOKC-TV news feature called *On the Spot!* She would pick up his story, interview him, and…WOKC-TV was no doubt affiliated with one of the major networks. By tomorrow, he would be back where he belonged, on the A-List of media elites!

CHAPTER 3

Though her efforts to confirm the Reillys' account of a fracas had, so far, been unproductive as trying to milk a bull, Henrietta continued to canvass the courthouse area for witnesses to Andrew Jackson Reilly's alleged assault and battery of a drum beater, and…

"Yes, I saw that crazy fat man make a fool of himself," said an elderly woman holding a Poodle dog in her arms. "He ought to be kept under lock-and-key for making all that racket. But no, there was no noticeable violence, not this time."

Hmmm.

"Yep, I watched the hootin'-'n'-hollerin'," said the old codger standing beside her with a cat in his arms. "Just ordinary carrying on by folks with nothin' better to do than play childish games of Cowboys-'n'-Indians."

Hmmm.

"My Happy Hour brunch bunch and I were at the 24/7 Hangout, heard the commotion and came a-runnin'," said a middle-aged, well-dressed fella carrying a briefcase, semi-recognizable as a local lawyer. "Handed out my cards, but haven't yet had anyone complain about criminal acts or personal injury."

Hmmm.

Just as she was silently complaining to her own self that no one seemed to have took pictures of the fracas reported by the Reillys…

"I recorded the whole thing for my sister who lives in Philadelphia, Pennsylvania," said another middle-aged fella. "Just lookee here," he said, holding up an iPhone that—dang it—showed nothing but video of his own grinning red face, as faintly in the background others could be heard chanting something about "poor old Kaw-Liga".

On the one hand, encouraged that the client's confrontations with a private citizen and a policeman might not have amounted to a hill of beans—but on the other hand, mindful that Andrew Jackson's word would likely not carry much water in a "urinating" contest with an aggravated cop—Henrietta gave up canvassing and headed down the block toward the 24/7 Happy Hours Hangout favored by members of the regular courthouse crowd.

Inside the country-and-western themed watering hole, more crowded and…

Ha, ha, ha, ha, ha, ha…

…rowdier than usual for lunchtime …

♫**Kaw-Liga was a wooden Indian standing by the door/ He fell in love with an Indian maiden over in the antique store…** ♫

…with everybody laughing and loud music playing on an old-fashioned juke box.

♫**He always wore his Sunday feathers and held a tomahawk/ The maiden wore her beads and braid, and hoped someday he'd talk…** ♫

In answer to her asking what was going on, a bartender explained that "the boys" were just celebrating memory of Oklmulgee's favorite native son, "ol' Mel McDaniel".

♫**Kaw-Liga, too stubborn to ever show a sign/ Because his heart was made of knotty pine…** ♫

"Ol' Mel is sorta the Happy Hours' patron saint," he added, with a nod of his ten-gallon-hatted head at a wooden plaque on the wall behind the bar with painted-on words that said:

"There's enough things in the world to keep you bummed out. My fans don't want to hear me sing something that's gonna bum 'em out more."

Mel McDaniel (1942 - 2011)

♫**Poor old Kaw-Liga, he never got a kiss/ Poor old Kaw-Liga, he don't know what he missed…** ♫

Henrietta turned to survey the hangout for others who might

have rushed out to see the earlier fracas involving Andrew Jackson and…

♫**Is it any wonder that his face is red/ Kaw-Liga, that poor old wooden head**♫

…spotted none other than Willis Willis…

Ha, ha, ha, ha, ha, ha…

…setting at a corner table with a semi-dark-skinned fella…

Ha, ha, ha, ha, ha, ha…

…and laughing his own head off along with the other "boys".

She went on over to the corner table, and… "Meet Roy Rector, Henrietta," said her boss, looking more sober, bright-eyed and cheerful than at anytime recently. "We're talking about a big lawsuit with potential to earn, uh, justice for Roy's oppressed people."

♫**Ever have a hot date, one of those that can't wait/ Things go a little too far…?**♫

"Can't share the details now, but…"

Her boss winked at Roy Rector and took a drink from a glass of darkish liquid that looked more like iced tea than Jim Barleycorn, then asked what was going on at the office.

♫**Stand up, if you ever been there/ Stand up, tell us all about it…**♫

Henrietta set down at the table and tried to explain…

Ha, ha, ha, ha, ha, ha…

…the legal trouble facing Andrew Jackson Reilly.

♫**Thought I was a he-man, do it just for me, man/ Knew just what to do…**♫

"I wouldn't worry about Ham Burger pressing serious charges at the arraignment," said Willis, referring to the District Attorney for Okmulgee County. "Not against anyone with a mama wearing a red MAGA cap."

♫**Thought I was a hero, she rated me a zero/ Said, "Honey, you ain't through ..**♫

Semi-relieved and feeling semi-cheerful her own self, Henrietta nodded at the new client, stood up from the 24/7 Happy Hours table and headed back to the office.

♫I said, stand up, have you ever been there?/ Stand up, identify/ Stand up, tell us all about it/ Stand up, testify ♫
Ha, ha, ha, ha, ha, ha…

CHAPTER 4

Andrew got up from his PlayStation console and, with his bowels more agitated than usual, began to pace the debris-littered floor of his basement man cave.

Though uncomfortable, his nervous and irritable bowels—symptoms of exposure to a world fraught with horrors— were a sign of refined taste. As noted by Montaigne, defecation was practiced by kings, philosophers, and even ladies. As observed by Swift, men were never so thoughtful as when at stool.

During the past two hours he had played the final episode of *Wolf Among Us* for at least the thousandth time, but…Despite knowing the game's characters and storylines by heart—and despite having reluctantly turned off his phone to avoid breaking news interruptions—he had again failed to make the right choices leading to a satisfying outcome.

Setting of the popular video game was a community of folklorian characters appearing as thinly disguised modern-day public figures, thanks to applications of magical "glamour" a/k/a media portrayals. As the player, he was theoretically in control of the game's mover-and-shaker, Bigby Wolf, a/k/a Donald Trump. In fact, however, the badass sheriff brought in to end the lunacy, chaos and bad taste that had Fabletown teetering on the edge of abyss was himself prone to unpredictable transformations from glamourized human identity to native wolf form and outbursts of lupine behavior.

Though "not as bad as everyone said" in the opinion of some, in fact many residents of the town did not trust Bigby, and resisted his efforts to both protect Fabletown characters from themselves and bring to justice the notorious loan shark and secretly criminal mastermind, the Crooked Man a/k/a George Soros.

Operating from behind the storefront of The Lucky Pawn a/k/a the Federal Reserve Bank…aided and abetted in production of black market glamours by his ruthlessly manipulative cohort, Bloody Mary a/k/a Hilary Clinton, and her deep-state henchmen—Dee and Dum Tweedle a/k/a ex-C.I.A. Director, John Brennan, and ex-F.B.I. Director, James Comey—the Crooked Man used blackmail to pull the strings controlling Fabletown's corrupt Acting Mayor from Sleepy Hollow, Ichabod Crane a/k/a Joe Biden.

Fellow gamers accurately described Crane as a corrupt, cowardly, spiteful, cruel, callous, arrogant, temperamental and egotistical political hack. One of the Fabletown characters told Crane to his face that he was "an asshole, who didn't give a shit about them." And near the end, the town's disgraced Acting Mayor—claiming that "the town took everything it could out of me"—admitted that he "took a little bit back in return."

Andrew barely resisted a powerful urge to turn on his phone and check for Hunter Biden alerts from his favored breaking news sources.

Yes, Bigby Wolf was also no Boy Scout. One of the town folk criticized him for "favoring rich fucks and ignoring the needs of others." But the sheriff had warned in advance that he was not going to change the way he did things, which in his own words was "being BIG and BAD." And he finally nailed Crane. But in the final episode titled *Cry Wolf*…after using his huff-and-puff powers to defeat Bloody Mary and a swarm of her clones a/k/a deep-state Clintonistas…then cornering the Crooked Man…

Faced with the option of having Bigby kill Soros or give in to the criminal mastermind's plea for a fair trial, Andrew had frozen at the PlayStation controls.

Hmmm.

Paused from pacing, he reached into his fridge.

Ymmm.

Restored by a few spoonfuls of cheese dip…

Seeking aid and comfort of fellow gamers, he returned to his desk, continued to resist a craving for breaking news, and turned on his laptop. In an Onanon.net chat room usually focused on game play, comments were being posted in unusually rapid succession. One-after-another, Andrew read:

I drove through Oklahoma one time and got cheated out of my lunch money at one of those Indian casinos.

They also rip off unsuspecting whites at their tax-free so-called smoke shops, which hooked me on the tobacco they started smuggling across the border in olden times.

Yeah, lots more whites have died from coughing than Indians who bit dust at that Wounded Knee fracas in South Dakota.

It's called genocide, guys. And as the white population continues to die off, the so-called Native American population has displaced us with an increase from only 556,000 in 1960 to 9.7 million in the 2020 Census.

We were warned. The white settlers on Roanoke Island disappeared after inviting Indians to have Thanksgiving dinner at the Plymouth Hard Rock and then disappeared, all eaten along with turkeys-'n'-fixins by redskins that went cannibalistic.

That's why George Washington wrote the Declaration of Independence, complaining that the government, quote, "had incited domestic insurrection amongst us, and endeavored to bring upon inhabitants of our frontiers"—meaning the red states—"the merciless Indian Savages, whose known rule of warfare is an undistinguished destruction of all ages and sexes."

Yeah, just like the Hamas tribe over there in our Holy land.

Indians also ganged up on Custer's troops, and massacred all of them. Someone wrote a sad song about it that my mother sang to me as a lullaby.

Better not drive through Oklahoma again, not since the damn Supreme Court ruled that the so-called sovereign Indian Nation reservations never got cancelled when Oklahoma became a state.

They don't believe in private property. They're all Communists.

They now have their own car tags! That's pure-dee unAmerican.

They're natives alright, but sure enough not Americans.

They'll take your lunch money and your scalp in Oklahoma!

I'm a drummer in our church choir, so I caught on to the message that the Indian chief wearing that wolf-head hat was sending on his tom-tom. The Creeks are fixing to go on the warpath, and soon.

Andrew began to feel unusually gaseous.

That Hells Angel wearing the motorcycle hat had balls. But the Creeks will likely roast his cohones in retaliation for his courageous stand in defense of our women and children.

And have his whole carcass for supper.

Andrew began to feel unusually nauseous.

He's an American hero in my book. We ought to start a GoFundMe campaign for the benefit of his wife and children.

And call in the Boogaloo militia to beat the shit out of those hungry savages!

Gentlemen, Andrew typed, *that was me — Old Hickory — who got arrested this morning for interrupting that distinctly unrhythmic drumbeat. I'm being hauled into court for assault and battery on Monday.*

We've got your back, Old Hick. Chances are that the Creeks will turn out to be Pretendians, and run for the hills.

Yeah, like Fauxchahontas a/k/a Elizabeth Warren, the left-winged Oklahoma blonde bitch who ran all the way to Massachusetts, gamed the system and took the Senate seat previously sat in by Sitting Bullshit Kennedy, hero of the Battle of Chappaquid<u>dick</u>.

Remember that college professor in Colorado who dined-out for years on false claims of being an Indian entitled to handouts? They caught onto his lies and ran his lily-white ass off the cushy reservation.

With his bowels in a uproar, Andrew turned on his phone… tapped into his usually most reliable breaking news source, but…ho-hum, read only a report that a cure for cancer had been discovered.

CHAPTER 5

Henrietta cracked open a can of beer, collapsed onto a living room divan, and clicked the remote controller of a television set. Onto the screen came the gray-whiskered face of Wolf Blitzer, who must have been setting in for the prettier-faced Kaitlan Collins. She had felt sorry for the young female news reader a year or two ago, when Steven Colbert introduced her as a star at CNN engaged in telling "fair and balanced news", causing the west coast studio audience theirselves to laugh out loud.

Henrietta sighed. As for why she her own self continued to watch and semi-listen to what was said on the original cable news channel, she couldn't rightly say.

In high school, she her own self had ambition to become a newspaper reporter and someday win one of those Pulitzer Prizes for writing something worth reading. Afterward, working at the now defunct local paper, the *Henryetta Weeky Herald*, she had started learning about journalism of the old-fashioned kind from Mr. Harold Mixon. The editor, publisher, and owner of the paper by inheritance was about the most educated person she had ever known. But had no stomach for telling bad news, which meant the "Weekly Harold"—as some called it—hardly reported any real news at all.

Promoted to Sports Editor—a job of all broth and no beans mainly requiring her to just write down scores of local kids' games that got called in—she had been instructed by Mr. Harold to just type "8 to 3" or "14 or 0" or whatever, and leave it at that, without telling whether Hornets or Wolves or Rattlesnakes had won or lost. "No need to reinforce the binary mindset that's already got us into a pickle," he'd said, before explaining that human brains had a tendency to take shortcuts in search of certainty about complex matters, and see things in simplified black-and-white terms such as all-or-nothing us-against-them.

And that was back in 2014, when voters soured on President Obama and a Tea Party won elections.

Her mentor would not tolerate mixing into news stories subjective points of view and personal opinions that some readers might have found either agreeable or disagreeable. Regarding controversial subjects that had folks already stirred up, he had repeatedly cautioned that people were inclined to infuse bad feelings about their own personal grievances into accounts of unrelated events involving other people, which he called "scapegoating".

Time and time again Mr. Harold had repeated a well known Cherokee Indian fable about everyone having two wolves inside theirselves—one good and the other bad—fighting each other for control. When asked by a young boy which wolf would win, a wise elder famously told him that "the wolf you feed" would overcome its rival.

As Wolf Blitzer continued to announce the latest "Breaking News" about something said or done by President Donald Trump, Henrietta recalled reading that many had doubted the notion of CNN's founder—a Mr. Ted Turner—that people would watch and listen to news all day every day or, for that matter, that there was enough news to fill seven days of twenty-four-hour airtime. And as things turned out, the doubters were half right, she reckoned. Cable news nowadays consisted almost entirely of predictable commentary, including lots of explanation of what really happened, lots of speculation about what could happen, and at least half the time…

Henrietta her own self had a low opinion of Donald Trump and would not have voted for him if held at gunpoint by Sean Hannity, but marveled that anyone would continue watch and listen to words and pictures put on by CNN's so-called journalists and expert contributors who had repeatedly cried wolf about the elected President's alleged collusion with Russia in countless "Bombshell" reports that had proved to be duds.

The Cable News Network had never apologized for wrongly putting the country through a divisive crisis. And to take the rag off the bush, continued to bring on expert commentators and unpaid guests that had proved to be unreliable as Pinocchio when it came to telling truth:

Two ex G-men, both fired by the F.B.I. for untruthful behavior... two so-called intelligence experts, who just before the 2020 election joined in a statement of other ex-intelligence officers in wrongfully declaring that reports of a politically embarrassing Hunter Biden laptop was a Russian attempt at spreading disinformation...and one of two disreputable lawyers who had already been put in jail for lying...had continued to show up on CNN to cater an ongoing feeding frenzy of viewers who couldn't get their fill of bad commentary about the re-elected President.

If a boyfriend had ever tried to dish out such bullshit over and over again, he would have long since been kicked off the divan and out of the house, Henrietta was thinking, when...

Dum-dum-dum-dum/ Dum-dum-dum-dum...

What in tarnation! Video of what looked to be today's local fracas involving Andrew Jackson Reilly came on the tv screen as...

"...still reeling from the attempted genocide of indigenous Palestinians in Gaza and Mexicans in Minneapolis," the voice of Wolf Blitzer was saying, "the world was shocked earlier today by an unprovoked white militia attack on the venerable leader of a tribe of Native Americans in the town square of Okmulgee, Oklahoma."

Uh oh.

"As the tribal elder shown peacefully pounding a tom-tom conducted a sacred ritual, the Hells Angel shown armored with a black motorcycle helmet broke from the white mob that encircled the old medicine man and...Watch in horror how the ugly scene unfolded."

Dum-dum-dum-dum…

As jerky video likely recorded by a handheld phone showed mainly bobbing headwear, including a Native American wolf-head hat…a black motorcycle helmet…and a red MAGA cap…

Dum-dum-dum…

"Stop the genocide!" a female voice among the whooping-and-hollering of others hollered.

"Many must have yelled 'From the river to the sea, the Creek Nation must be free!' Wolf Blitzer's voice added.

Dum-dum…

"Later identified as a local white supremacist named Andrew Jackson Reilly, the cowardly attacker was arrested by police, but then released into the frightened community where the Creek Nation is headquartered. Needless to say, tensions remain high," said Blitzer when his whiskered face came back onto half of a split-screen along with a picture of a familiar dark-haired gal holding a microphone in front of her face.

"Our always on-the-spot reporter, Christiane Amanpour, reached out to the attacker for a confession, but…Tell us what lies you encountered, Christiane."

Uh oh.

"The attacker cowered in an underground hideout, but I was able to interrogate his mother and—get this, Wolfie—the obviously inebriated old white woman, proudly flaunting a red MAGA cap, claimed that her son is 'part-Indian' himself, and was entitled to have a turn at pounding the tribe's ceremonial drum. She says she is 'proud' of her 'boy'."

Dang.

"Yes, typical misplaced MAGA maternal malice," said "Wolfie", now shown setting next to an oldish, pigtailed fellow wearing a headband with a feather stuck in it. "Here with us in studio to provide context of the eruption of white hate in a near repeat of the massacre of innocent Native American women and children at Wounded Knee, is Professor Ward Churchill," the veteran CNN anchorman announced. "As a Native American himself, former head of the affirmative action office and professor of ethnic studies at the University of Colorado—plus author of several bombshells about continued attempts by whites to 'Americanize' Native Americans out of existence—Professor Churchill is a genocide expert. Welcome, Professor."

"Wa-Do, my friend, Lobo," said the expert. "Indeed, I have walked the walk with my brothers and sisters across this land on an unending trail of salty tears. And talked the talk in several bookstores that carried my works that are still available on the cheap at Amazon. In a nutshell, alas, gone are the days when my people sensibly brought their livestock into federal housing."

"Yes, but despite relentless pressure to give up traditional ways, your people have continued to resist genocidal assimilation into white man's society by removing unhygienic toilets from their living quarters and putting unsanitary toilets outside."

"The continuing peril of genocide my people face is not only indoor plumbing and cowardly attacks such as took place today in Oklahoma," said the Native American book writer. "An even greater threat is continued sexual mixing with whites."

"Yes, rape is a common tactic employed by marauding white men," said Blitzer. "Their penises are as viciously lethal as cavalry rifles."

"Not just white dicks, Lobo. Anglo women—especially after a few shots of firewater—find red men such as myself irresistible."

Dang it, Andrew Jackson's alleged assault and battery of an elderly Native American might qualify as an especially serious so-called "hate crime"—legally worse than beating-up someone just for the fun of it—likely to stir up…

Disgusted by the inflammatory CNN coverage of today's event that eyeball-witnesses had barely noticed—plus worried about the effect of unfavorable publicity on treatment of her client—Henrietta clicked off the picture of Wolf Blitzer's hairy face, jumped up from the divan, and went to the kitchen for another can of beer.

CHAPTER 6

♫*Headin' out on some uncharted path/ It happens time and time again/ You never seem to reach the end…* ♫

With an old song favored by her late Grandma O'Hara running through her mind, likely due to a combination of worries, Henrietta drove her old Checker cab of a car into an Okmlgee neighborhood of rundown houses. Worry about what she had read yesterday about addictions…about her own self following in the footsteps of Willis Willis…about the video of the incident involving Andrew Jackson Reilly spreading the story of a white man committing genocide…

♫*Suddenly, the pressure's fallin', fallin'/ Skies have all turned gray/ Suddenly, the storm is headed straight your way…* ♫

To boot, she worried about CNN's crafty Christine Amanpour getting the client's mother to talk on tv. Though the District Attorney might ordinarily be not inclined to press charges against the son of a MAGA mama, if the D.A. felt overwhelmed by media pressure…

♫*It's like a full force gale/ Atop a mountain of cold/ You tell your story again and again/ And it never gets old…* ♫

Henrietta hoped to get favorable information about the unusual "boy" from his own self, to put in front of old Judge Dwight at the arraignment in District Court on Monday and maybe get lenient treatment of her client. But even if Andrew Jackson turned out to be a singer in a church choir…Sure enough, several tv station vans were parked out front of the Reillys' ramshackle residence.

♫*You face a wall of mirrors/ You charge 'em at full speed/ You cover up, you hear shattering glass/ But you never bleed/ You never feel the need...* ♫

After wading through a gaggle of tv camera crews, reporters holding microphones, and others no doubt assigned to jotting stories for print publications, she knocked on the house's front door and...

"Well, well, our tongue-tied mouthpiece," said Irene Reilly, caked with face make-up, her reddish hair curled, and wearing what was no doubt her Sunday-best house dress. "Come in and join us for refreshments and conversation."

Inside a not very tidy living room...What in Sam Hill! Getting up from a ratty divan was none other than Ms. Katie Couric—reportedly now a news podcaster, and still a wolf in sheep clothes if there ever was one—who then skulked out the door without a word of continued "conversation".

"Dang it, Miz Reilly, on the phone last night I advised against you and your 'boy' telling anything more to anyone about the fix he's in."

"Andrew Jackson locked hisself in the basement and wouldn't say nothin', not even after Katie tried to break down the door with a sledgehammer. All she wanted to know about was his political views."

"Except for him calling ex-President John Kennedy a 'tool', you said he didn't have no political opinions."

"Well, he don't vote, and keeps up with news partly because he don't like any politician. And I don't neither. I dredged this 'MAGGOT' hat out of a garbage can at the Goodwill store."

Hmmm.

"But it would have been rude of me not to offer Katie refreshment, then just set there on the divan like a bump on a log."

Henrietta stomped a foot and insisted on talking directly to Andrew Jackson.

"He won't talk to anyone when he's playing games with hisself, which is almost always," said the mother. "He says opening the door to his room is lit'rally opening a box of Pandora cigars."

Dum…Dum…Dum…

"That's my boy now, taking a break from playing that video game and pounding on his set of drums for relief of excitement that upsets his bowels."

Dum…Dum…

Down a flight of creaking wood stairs, Henrietta knocked extra hard on a door and…

Dum…

…hollered for the client to open up unless he wanted to be dragged out of his playpen in handcuffs by a deputy sheriff on Monday.

The door opened and her client, standing there in red pajamas with attached booties, one earflap of a billed green hunting cap pulled down and the other up, with what looked to be potato-chip crumbs mixed with traces of *Cheez-Whiz* imbedded in his mangy beard…

"I don a motorcycle helmet when forced to venture into the wild, but otherwise eschew handcuffs, anklets, necklaces, dental braces, rings or other metal attachments to any part of my person since Robert Kennedy, Junior alerted us to the effects of food in cans," he declared.

Inside the dimly lit "man cave", Henrietta informed the, uh, unusual person that a media storm about his involvement in yesterday's, uh "incident" would likely, uh, complicate his arraignment and…

"Yes, I know. My paranoia is not completely out of control," he said, before a ping prompted him to look at his phone.

"As a youngun, Andrew Jackson delighted in greeting me with bad news when I got home from work," said his mama. "Roof leaking, furnace blowed up…the worse the disaster, the more pleasure he took in telling about it. Later, he went off to college to learn how to read news like the famous tv anchorman, Ron Burgundy. But big shots at the stations in Tulsa said he didn't have the face for radio or the voice for tv, and had wrong opinions about everything."

"Suspicion of a mass shooting in Chicago," the would-be

anchorman announced after looking up from his phone. "Early reports of multiple dead bodies found at a mortuary. And a Cook County D.A. has charged Trump with felony jaywalking while setting up the massacre of likely undocumented immigrants during a recent clandestine visit to the Windy City."

Asked to tell what led to the scuffle with an elderly Native American yesterday right there in Okmulgee, Oklahoma…

"The old person beating that drum was hopelessly out of rhythm, requiring that I take matters in hand and correct the beat," he answered. "But back to the media storm about me: In the approximate words of my possibly distant Cousin Ignatius, though only the universe and human stupidity are infinite, it's amazing that any hack could pen such atrocious melodrama. Unfortunately, people are most apt to believe what they least understand, according to Montaigne, and inclined to be more certain, confident, resolute, disdainful and grave than donkeys."

"To help me my own self persuade old Judge Dwight to believe you are not a bad person…"

"Again according to Montaigne, 'Life itself is neither good nor evil, but rather where good or evil find a place, depending upon how you make it for them.'"

That bit of ancient wisdom from overseas sounded a lot like the Cherokee fable about two wolves inside people that Mr. Harold had often told, Henrietta reckoned But …

Ping.

Andrew Jackson again looked at his phone, appeared to read another news alert, then announced that a "dew point" indicated that unseasonably cold, dry air from the Rocky Mountains was violently colliding with warm, moist air from the Gulf of Mexico as a result of climate change passing a "tipping point", and could cause a devastating outbreak of life-threatening tornados across the Plains, but…

"Montaigne, who virtually invented the art of essay as a literary *genre*, famously said that his life had been full of terrible misfortunes, most of which never happened. He, however, lived in relatively civilized times, and was lucky. Nowadays, mankind's position in the universe is pure misery, with no reason for optimism. As during the times of Jonathan Swift, we are currently beset with reports of conspiracies, rebellions, massacres, revolutions, and banishments caused by faction, ambition and hypocrisy that nurtures widespread madness, malice, hatred and rage."

Ping.

Hmmm.

Mention of a Jonathan Swift brought to mind a book assigned in high school that told of foreigners thinking that a stranger's pocket watch must have been an "oracle", on account of him repeatedly consulting it and explaining that it pointed out the time for everything he did.

Sure enough, her client then passed on news that a transgender Democrat in Washington had "taken a shot" at the president of the Allstate Insurance Company for failure to protect the country against a Mr. Mayhem.

"I'm your lawyer, Mr. Reilly, sworn to be confidential about what you say," said Henrietta. "So tell me, did you happen to be on or off any, uh, 'medicine' yesterday that might've, uh, diminished your brain capacity when you and the off-beat Native American drummer…?"

"If you're 'round about asking if I was spurred into action by dopamine, the answer of course is yes."

Aha.

"My boy has a brain undiminished as all outdoors inside that melon-size head of his," said Irene Reilly.

"Yesterday's unseemly aural spectacle did indeed cause my bowels to rumble more excitedly than usual," said the boy, "in reaction to a gigantic release of dopamine from my enormous brain, as is usual when one is aroused with anger. It was Mother Nature's way of stirring me to act as an avenging sword of taste and decency."

Hmmm.

"If you're hiding down there, Andrew Jackson Reilly, better show yourself with hands up," someone hollered from above.

Henrietta followed Ms. Reilly from the room and—as the door to the man cave slammed behind them—hurried up the creaky stairs, where…What in tarnation! A fella wearing the all-black uniform of the Creek Nation's Police Department of "Lighthorsemen" was standing at the top of the stairs with hands on his hips, there—he said—to execute a warrant for Andrew Jackson's arrest on charges of yesterday's assault, and take the accused into custody.

Henrietta introduced herself as attorney for the accused, told the Lighthorseman that her client had already been charged for the alleged offense by Okmulgee police, and was due to be arraigned in Okmulgee County District Court on Monday morning.

"You're tryin' to get my boy into double-bubble trouble, which is against his constitution," Irene Reilly rightly complained, but…

"Nope," the Native American policeman replied. "Under the U.S. Supreme Court ruling in *Sharp v. Murphy* following the *McGirt* decision confirming sovereignty of the Indian Nations of Oklahoma, our court has jurisdiction to prosecute crimes committed by members of the Creek Nation. And according to numerous news reports, Andrew Jackson Reilly qualifies. A Preliminary Hearing is set for two-thirty this afternoon."

Henrietta stomped a foot. Dang it, a tribal prosecutor and judge were not likely to go easy on anyone who—by the look of things—had in fact committed assault and battery against a tribal elder engaged in a sacred Native American ceremony.

CHAPTER 7

Unbathed, unbshaved, and utterly undone in the aftermath of an unhinged 18-hour hissy fit, Don Melone stared at the super-sized tv screen mounted to a wall in his smallish apartment.

Sharing his *Rednecks vs. Redskins* video reort with Peg Patterson at WOKC-TV in Oklahoma City had been professionally rash. Instead of having him zoom onto her usually inane so-called news show called *On the Spot,* the way past-her-prime two-timing bitch had both locally aired and passed on to her station's network his Storytime Guy breaking news with… with his voice-over erased! Worldwide media had run with the Pulitzer Prize-worthy piece of investigative journalism without…without mention of his authorship!

And to add insult to injury, thirty seconds ago ABC had teased that *The View's* regular *Friday Flashback* feature would focus on what it called the current repeat of a prior ugly incident involving a Native American elder and Kentucky high schooler that took place at the Lincoln Memorial in 2019.

Damnit, the daily display of female hot flashes by supposedly post-menopausal females had been launched by that lisping bitch who couldn't even pronounce her own name — Babbling Babwa Walters — as "a talk show featuring four or five women who would discuss topics of the day, mixing humor with intelligent debate." To his amazement and chagrin, the *New York Times* had puffed up the *Bobble Heads R Us* production by deeming fit to print that it was "the most important political tv show in America." And now…

Sure enough, after showing *The View's* set — backdropped

by a panorama of the Big Apple skyline that made his mouth water—a brief snippet of his video flashed by with a stranger's voice-over almost word-for-word matching his Onanon.net version, without attribution! To raucous, probably canned studio audience applause, onto the set came ABC's dopy daytime divas in what could have been a parade of contestants in an Ugly Queen Pageant:

Joy Behar, a former unfunny so-called stand-up comedienne dating back to the days of Vaudeville by all appearances. She was the nobody cast to provide interesting commentary because, according to Babwa, Joy would "say anything".

Whoopi Goldberg, the also aged, balding former actress, who had admitted to wedding a Hebrew man in hopes of getting a break in Hollywood. With that credential solely to her adopted Jewish name, Whoopi had famously opined that the Holocaust was "not racial".

Ana Navarro, nominally a Republican and obvious DEI hire, who to her credit—when caught making a blatantly false statement about nonexistent historical precedent for Biden's pardon of his bad boy's crimes—had flipped-off MAGA critics by telling them to "take it up with ChatGPT".

As Don ground his teeth…

"Today's Hot Topic is the brutal assault against a venerable leader of the Creek tribe of Native Americans living peacefully in Oklahoma, caught on camera by an on-the-spot reporter at our Oklahoma City affiliate," said Joy. "And we are honored to have with us the victim of the attempted genocide who miraculously survived the MAGA attack, Chief Kaw-Liga."

To the sound of more raucous applause, the old drumbeater—still wearing a mangy fur cape and the snarling toothy wolf-head hat—squeezed himself into a chair set between the big fat asses of Behar and Goldberg. Asked about the symbolic meaning of his Native American moniker, the Chief said he had heard about "Kaw-Liga" in an ancient song about a statue of a cigar store Indian, and reclaimed the name and title as part of his endeavor to restore and preserve his tribe"s traditional ways.

"Very interesting," said Joy in a thoughtful tone of voice, with a hand raised to support her chins in the manner of the famous statue called "The Thinker".

"And inspirational," Whoopi added. "I was proud to see that the Black brothers and sisters from my tribe had your back in the face-off with that drunken rabble of racist rednecks."

"Actually, the rednecks were surprisingly cheerful, not threatening, and in fact seemed to be supportive of my protest against a recent Supreme Court decision that…"

"Aha, fascist Republican judges doing Trump's dirty work again," said Ana. "Taking away your right to American citizenship and obligation to vote for Democrats in gratitude for getting free veneers on your immigrant peoples' teeth."

"Actually, it was the Creek Nation's own Supreme Court that overthrew our sacred tradition of limiting tribal citizenship under a longstanding 'Indians-by-Blood Rule', and dictated that we accept Creek Freedmen."

"Freedmen?" said Joy, clueless as ever. "Surely, you do not mean to say that noble Indians were among the mob of MAGA savages pardoned by Trump for their crime of insurrection."

To the dismay of the bitch brigade — and Don's delight — Chief Kaw-Liga went on to explain that in their ancestral Deep South homeland the Creeks had enslaved Africans…had brought the black-skinned people with them to Oklahoma…and had fought on the side of the Confederacy in the Civil War…but that in the wake of centuries of inter-marriage, so-called Creek Freedmen of part African descent had recently won entitlement to the goodies of tribal citizenship by Supreme Court edict.

"You were beating a drum and threatening judges?!" said Whoopi, obviously outraged by the cultural appropriation of Senator Schumer's intimidation tactic.

"The thug in the helmet and bullet-proof vest was an ICE agent, trying to deport Freedmen and their families to Africa?!" said an equally outraged Ana Navarro.

"And deport Native Americans to…to where?" Joy Behar

sputtered. "I've heard your people are mongoloids who originally came from China, but with Trump's terrible tariffs in force…"

As a commercial for *Black Cohosh Root* abruptly came onto the screen—promising to reduce hormonal imbalance, hot flashes and night sweats—Don grudgingly admitted to himself that he'd missed the ICE optics created by Andrew Jackson Reilly's apparel that would have guaranteed a more horrified and angrier outpouring of upward thumbs from his Storytime Guy followers. And no doubt intensified anti-Trump sentiment in the hungry minds of a broader audience that should have been his! But…

With the tv clicked off, Don stared at the blank screen and, figuratively speaking, licked his chops. He would be no one's bitch. As a proud gay man who knew a thing or two about dog-eating-doggie, he would forego catty hissing-and-scratching retaliation on his Onanon channel, loose his inner wolf, and start biting.

CHAPTER 8

♫Living on Tulsa time/ Living on Tulsa time/ Well you know that I've been through it/ when I set my watch back to it/ Living on Tulsa time…♫

With the Checker's radio tuned to the hourly *News in a Nutshell* broadcasted by a Tulsa station, Henrietta drove toward the Creek Nation's headquarters, a so-called Mound Building said to have been named and shaped in remembrance of hills of piled-up dirt used in olden times as ceremonial platforms and tribal administrative hubs.

On the one hand, she was relieved to have found that under Creek law the maximum penalty Alexander Jackson Reilly faced for even hateful assault and battery could not be more three years in jail, compared to worse possibilities he would have faced under Oklahoma law in Oklmulgee County District Court. On the other hand, whereas the District Attorney, Ham Burger, might have been inclined toward favorable treatment of the son of a "MAGA mama", a Creek Nation prosecutor, het-up about…

"In the aftermath of yesterday's racially-charged incident in Okmulgee that interrupted public celebration of the 1814 defeat of a band of so-called 'Red Sticks'," said the radio news announcer, "the only recently liberated Creek 'Freedmen' continue to fight against the blatantly racist effort of Neo-Red Sticks to restore 'traditional tribal 'ways', by earlier today filing a lawsuit against the Creek Nation in tribal court."

Hmmm.

"The tribe's powers-that-be have revealed themselves to be 'Indian givers', according to crusading civil rights attorney, Willis

V. Willis…"

Uh oh.

"… by not living up to their own Supreme Court decision of three years ago that finally recognized the entitlement of Black Freedmen's descendants to full enjoyment of tribal citizenship and attendant benefits."

Hmmm.

"The lawsuit comes in the wake of yesterday's ugly incident in Okmulgee sparked by Neo-Nazi rabble-rousers that harkens bitter memories created by recent reports of a shameful 1921 genocidal massacre committed by white supremacists that destroyed the Greenwood neighborhood of Tulsa and took the lives of twenty-six descendants of African-American slaves brought to Oklahoma by the Creeks and other Civilized Tribes.

"And yet, Creek tribal authorities have vindictively lodged criminal charges against Andrew Jackson Reilly, the courageous defender of social justice who peacefully pushed-back against a 'Chief' Kaw-Liga's hateful rhetoric aimed at stirring up another racial massacre."

♫Well you know that I've been through it/ When I set my watch back to it/ Living on Tulsa time♫

Dang it, though indirectly defending their client, Willis' lawsuit—coupled with local broadcast of another side of the story—was likely to have further stirred up both tribal "powers that be" and…Sure enough, a crowd had been drawn like cats to catnip and dogs to red meat by tv news vans parked out front of the Mound Building.

Some were holding up signs mounted on white sticks, while shouting, "ICE agents are enforcing law!" and such. Others held up signs on red sticks, while hollering, "ICE agents are Nazis!" and such.

It took more than thirty minutes for Henrietta to get through the rowdy mob and a security checkpoint into the Mound, that inside—except for being newish, modern, and decorated with Native American emblems mainly featuring animals—looked about like the county courthouse. Same for a courtroom, packed with onlookers and no doubt more reporters, where...

Already setting at a table in the courtroom well was Andrew Jackson, back to wearing his motorcycle helmet, along with a heavy flannel shirt, sweat pants and flip-flops on account of having no suit, tie and shoes. And already setting on the courtroom bench was a judge wearing a black robe just like old Judge Dwight in District Court.

Without mentioning that she was working for Willis V. Wills, Henrietta introduced herself as attorney for the Defendant.

"Objection!" someone shouted from behind her, and... into the well like a blast of hot air came District Attorney Hamilton "Ham" Burger, waving a fist, then turning around to face...a tv camera in the rear that she'd not previously noticed... and declaring: "Jurisdiction for maintaining law and order in Okmulgee County resides with the State of Oklahoma, represented by me!"

"Not when the criminal offender is a citizen of the Creek Nation," a fella who looked to be a tribal prosecutor answered.

"That scoundrel sitting there in chains is no more Native American than Elizabeth 'Lieawatha' Warren," said Burger, referring to the Oklahoma gal who had gone on to become a U.S. Senator for Massachusetts by, some said, gaming the DEI system.

"Point taken, Mr. Burger," said the judge, but in this case..."

Henrietta her own self had scoffed at the *New York Times* judgement that DNA tests indicating that Ms. Warren was between 1.56% and 0.024% Native American proved she was telling the truth about being Native American. But what mostly irritated her own self was that the Senator claimed that she—as a blonde-haired youngun growing up in Oklahoma—had suffered from hateful racial discrimination. In fact—correctly or not—almost everyone in Oklahoma <u>boasted</u> of being part Indian.

Heck, the state's still most beloved native son—Will Rogers—was a member of the Cherokee tribe, as were one of Oklahoma's two recent U.S. Senators and a Governor.

Creek authorities had "expedited a Preliminary Hearing in order to put to the test a *prima facie* case against Mr. Reilly pending official determination of his citizenship status and, "hopefully calm waters surrounding the Nation," the judge was saying, which…

Hmmm.

…sounded like he might be eager to dismiss charges and disassociate his tribe from "Chief Kaw-Liga" and yesterday's "incident".

"The Defendant's mother publicly claims he's Creek by birth, and that's *prima facie* for practical purposes," said the prosecutor, apparently referring to Irene Reilly's media declarations. "A mama oughta know."

"Let's get her in the witness box and hear what the mama has to say under oath and peril of perjury," the D.A. bellowed.

Quick as a tick jumping onto the ear of a hound dog, Ms. Reilly bounded from the gallery into the well…took the stand and—smiling at the tv camera— testified that her real name was Peg. "My boy calls me 'Irene' because I gave him the name I saw on a statue down in New Orleans."

In a whisper, Henrietta advised Andrew Jackson, seated beside her, to stop fidgeting like he had a case of so-called DTs, and pay attention.

"Tell us about the ethnic or, if you will, racial family tree of your son," said the Creek Nation lawyer, "starting with his parentage."

"Like my possibly distant cousin and role model, Ignatius," the son semi-whispered. "I suspect my conception occurred in a rather offhand manner."

"Well, I myself am pure-dee Scotch, Irish and American, but as for Andrew Jackson's daddy, I can't rightly say what or even who he was," said the mama…

Ha, ha, ha…

…drawing both audible snickers and a burst of outright laughing by from gallery onlookers.

Further grilled about the basis of her claim that her boy was

Native American, the mama said that Ms. Katie Couric had led her to agree that he was a member a lost tribe of Jews turned Christian. And to admit that she had took her boy to church services once or twice.

Though unnecessary as socks on a rooster in summertime to undermining the reliability of Ms. Reilly's testimony, District Attorney Burger insisted on cross-examining the witness. When she told that Andrew Jackson had started howling like a wild Indian at birth, and as a toddler took to pounding on pans and washtubs like they were drums…

"Beating drums and chanting ♫Wig-wam bam sham-a-lam/ / Gonna get you if I can? ♫ the D.A. sarcastically semi-sang.

"Well, somethin' like that."

"Beating drums like a half-breed and chanting ♫We weren't accepted and I felt ashamed/ Nineteen I left them, tell me who's to blame?♫

"Well, yes, mean treatment by others must be the reason for how Andrew Jackson turned out."

"Dancing with wolves and chanting ♫Don't hand me no old peace pipe/ There ain't no pipe can settle the fight?♫

"Andrew Jackson don't dance, but…Well, when Ms. Megyn Kelly came around and said, 'Isn't it true my boy is a pretendian out to get benefits of tribal membership'…I have to get handed-down clothes at the Goodwill Store, and…I've got the arthritis in my hips that needs treatment-for-free by a medicine man. I wasn't gonna set there like a bump on a log."

Since the District Attorney seemed to suspect that Peg a/k/a Irene Reilly was a "pretend" MAGA mama—and her boy therefore not likely to be looked upon favorably by most county voters—Henrietta had stayed quiet about the Creek prosecutor's claim of jurisdiction. And sure enough…

Turning to again face the tv camera, Ham Burger bellowed: "What we have here is another All-American boy who's been turned against traditional ways by fake news, and turned by homosexual propaganda spouted by MSNOW into thinking he's a 'victim' of decent white Christian society who's entitled to coddlement. In District Court, I'll send him off to ten years at hard labor in state prison, where he's likely to get a red ass alright, but no 'gender-affirming' care provided at taxpayer expense!"

Ohhh the gallery onlookers ohhhed.

"You've made your point, Mr. Burger," said the judge, again sounding like he hisself would like to hand the case over to Oklahoma authorities, but... "While the Court takes the jurisdictional issue under advisement pending examination of tribal records, let's hear and tentatively consider the Attorney General's proffer of evidence of the Defendant's alleged offense."

Ohhh....

CHAPTER 9

Andrew sighed.

His alleged mother's failure to explain his actions had left him in the jaws of the so-called justice system controlled by those who, as observed by Swift, were bred in the art of proving, by words multiplied for the purpose, that white is black and black is white. And equally disposed to pervert the general reasoning of mankind to serve any cause for which they were paid. Outside their own trade, lawyers, and judges—those grown, old fat and lazy—were indeed the most ignorant and stupid among us.

As if to grafically illustrate Swift's point, the Creek Nation prosecutor set on persecuting him clicked a gadget that made the always inappropriately smirking face of MSNOW's Rachel Maddow come onto an exposed wall. As video silently played...

"Yesterday, the elderly man shown wearing a wolf headdress ..."

"Objection, Your Honor!" his strawberry-blonde lawyerette hollered. "The video without context of sound is misleading."

"You want 'context', I'll give you context," the prosecutor replied, and...

"Just when you thought Donald Trump and his murderous MAGA maniacs had sated their voracious appetite for innocent lambs' blood in Gaza and Minneapolis, get a load of this attempted slaughter of a Native American elder that took place in Okmulgee, Oklahoma," the famous female news announcer said in her tasteless, bright-eyed, always chirpy delivery of anarchist doxy, for which she deserved to be impaled on the member of a particularly large stallion. "The obviously straight white supremacist male shown waving a stick resembling a blood-engorged penis at the venerable Chief of the Creek Nation is Andrew Jack…"

"Objection, Your Honor! That inflammatory rhetoric by Ms. Maddow is unreliable hearsay," his lawyerette exclaimed. "My client was waving a plain ol' red-handled drumstick."

Andrew was now fully convinced that the obviously uneducated petticoated pettifogger beside him was grossly incapable of grasping the simple issues at play. As observed by Montaigne, the greater part of the world's troubles were due to grammar, a truth exemplified by Swift's account of Lemuel Gulliver's encounter with squabbling members of a tribe of Blefuscans, fiercely fighting one another—at a cost of millions of lives—over whether "flesh be bread" or "bread be flesh".

"For complete context, let's hear Ms. Maddow's expert hearsay in its entirety," the Creek Nation prosecutor shouted.

"She's a lying bitch!" someone else shouted, "so blinded by narrow ideology that she doesn't see the big picture."

Ohhh…

"So clever with words that even she doesn't understand what she says!"

Ohhh…

"So driven by personal ambition, she steals the fruits of others' labor, namely mine!"

Ohhh…

"But only I can provide complete context of yesterday's incident."

Though the somewhat dark-skinned mulatto entering the well was unusually disheveled in appearance and wearing a bathrobe, Andrew recognized him as Don Melone, the former cable guy who—among other scoops— had struck terror in the hearts and minds of viewers by astutely speculating that a missing Malaysian Airlines plane had been sucked into a black hole during a flight above the Indian Ocean.

Andrew looked forward to seeing and hearing what Melone would show and tell about the unseemly drumming duel that he would have preferred to settle as gentlemen at twenty paces, but…

As legal argle-bargle about acceptability of evidence offered by the veteran newsbreaker ensued —along with rumbling of his stomach—he was reminded that excessive consumption of processed cheese had been linked to suicidal thoughts, driving and operating machinery while asleep, and risk of compulsive behavior. But before he could pass on the warning…

"Bailiff, put Mr. Melone's thumb into… or rather, his thumb drive into that gadget for the court to see his firsthand video evidence," the judge ordered.

♫That famous day in history/ the men of the Seventh Cavalry went riding on/ And from the rear a voice was heard… ♫

A series of pictures of the Creek Nation's architectural erections appeared on the wall. By loud live voice-over of his recorded voice-over, Melone explained that he had captured yesterday's misreported incident on his phone in a <u>horizontal</u> format and—as wobbly pictures of yesterday's crowd appeared—that he had posted the video on his Storytime Guy channel at Onanon.net.

"That's another damn Tik Tok outlet of vicious lies used by China to stir up Communist discontent in America," the snarling District Attorney protested, though in fact the old Indian was accurately shown beating a drum, hopelessly out of rhythm with the beat of…

♫Poor old Kaw-Liga, he never got a kiss/ Poor old Kaw-Liga, he don't know what he missed… ♫

Ohhh…

The video had been picked up by national news media in its narrow vertical Onanon format, Melone further explained, with the result of focusing attention on the "scuffle" that broke out….

♫Is it any wonder that his face is red/ Kaw-Liga that poor old wooden head♫

…but eliminating the wider horizontal "context" showing that, in fact, it was a sub-group of agitators—holding up FREE FREEDMEN placards mounted on white sticks, shouting "Kaw-Liga is Racist!"—that got others in the crowd onto a warpath.

Ohhh…

Bang!

"The court is quite familiar with 'Chief Kaw-Liga'," said the judge after banging his gavel. "He is well known to use inflammatory rhetoric in opposition to our Supreme Court's recognition of Creek Freedmen's tribal citizenship and entitlement to cheap car tags."

Ohhh…

"The unfortunate fact remains, however, that the accused—whatever his motive—is clearly shown striking the old fool, who—though misguided—was entitled to protest for media attention and, uh, focus, without interruption by the Defendant."

Ohhh…

On top of that turn of misfortune, Andrew worried about breaking news of a catfight between Kris Kardashian and her publicity-shy daughters—sparked by the bashful babes' qualms about defecating on-camera—that was bound to bitterly divide devotees of America's First Family.

CHAPTER 10

Henrietta was undecided as a goat standing on a patch of green shag carpet.

On the one hand, her lawyerly duty was to defend Andrew Jackson Reilly against the criminal charges against him. On the other hand, she had a hunch that the judge was now thinking—along with her own self—that her client might be better off in Creek Nation jail than in District Court, if not best off in the care of a different kind of institution.

After whispered consultation with the client his own self, however, she reckoned she had to go along with his insistence to be put in the witness box to tell his version of yesterday's "news".

Asked by a bailiff to tell the truth, the whole truth and nothing but the truth, Andrew Jackson said that after studying Meteorology in college he had got a Master's Degree for how to talk like a tv anchorman. "Onscreen weathermen are rock stars in the State of Oklahoma," he said. "As demonstrated by Al Gore, when it comes to arousing widespread frission—the thrilling, chilling blend of excitement and recreational fear—Mother Nature's threats trump the hourly reports of conspiracies, rebellions, murders, massacres, revolutions and banishments said by Swift to be the effects of avarice, faction, hypocrisy, perfidiousness, cruelty, rage, madness, hatred, envy lust, malice and ambition. Indeed, as noted by Montaigne, fear is the strongest of passions."

Ohhh...the gallery of onlookers ohhhed.

"And you're now over thirty years of age, still living in your boyhood basement, and currently unemployed due to demands of looking after your unhealthy mama, right?"

"I do some dusting. And yes, Mother is quite demanding. Her pleas for emergency medical attention regularly interrupt my efforts to bring the *Wolf Among Us* to a satisfactory conclusion."

"By 'the wolf among us', you mean a certain video game that you sometimes play, right?"

"The five or six-hours-a-day I typically spend at the PlayStation controller provide me with a sense of agency in relation to current events. Additional daily hours in the company of other Wolfies in an Onanon chat room are of further assistance to staying on top of breaking news. And by the way, citing discovery of mummified human remains in Gaza, editors of the *New York Times* section for entertainment news are calling for the Pope's head on a platter, along with erasure of the Easter Bunny from kindergarten books. My bowels are in an uproar about possible cancelation of next year's parade."

Hmmm.

Disturbed her own self that Andrew Jackson—jumpy as a long-tailed cat in a roomful of rocking chairs—would continue to blurt echoes of "breaking news" out of the blue, Henrietta nevertheless decided to keep on trying to make him look less odd and more sympathetic to the judge.

"Yes, I suffer from both nervous and irritable bowel syndromes," he said in answer to her next question. "The condition results from exposure to the horrors of the century in which we are doomed to exist, as metaphorically documented by *Wolf Among Us* and more prosaically reported by news media."

"And you find relief by beating on drums, ain't that right?" said, Henrietta edging deeper into the context of her client's involvement in yesterday's incident.

"Yes, I practice percussion in preference to ingestion of *Pepto-Bismol* that is laced with droppings of bat guano according to taste tests personally conducted by Dr. Oz."

"As a drum-beating, possibly part-Native American medicine man your own self, and eyeball witness to goings-on out front of the county courthouse yesterday…"

"The scene was fraught with argument as heated as the dispute between Big-endians-versus-Little-endians reported by Jonathan Swift. The latter group, as you may recall…"

Henrietta stomped a foot and told the client to just provide the judge with his own plainspoke version of what happened yesterday, but…

"I myself subscribe to the Big-endian view that boiled eggs should be cracked at the larger end, but…"

Ohhh…

"…having studied how to be a tv news anchorman, I eschew the voicing of subjective personal accounts," said the witness, who then straightened up in the box, looked toward the tv camera, and…

"As the legendary anchorman, Ron Burgundy, would have put it," he continued, "a hopelessly unrhythmic drummer enraged a public gathering of recently freed Creek Negroes…"

Ohhh!

"'Negroes'?"

"When referring to people of dark-skinned African heritage I use the more elegant French term in preference to the pejorative word 'Black' that in common parlance carries with it derogatory connotations—'black-hatted', 'black-hearted', 'black-balled', etcetera—that contribute to sadomasochistic enjoyment of both collective victimhood by some and collective guilt by others."

Ohhh…

"In fact, it is modern-day extreme liberty that currently enslaves people of all races by encouraging self-indulgent behavior that becomes addictive."

Ohhh…

"What you mean to say is that descendants of African-Americans called Creek Freedmen were agitated by a 'Chief Kaw-Liga' drumming up support for restoration of ancient tribal ways, right?"

"A passerby, later identified as Andrew Jackson Reilly offered instruction to the wooden-headed Native American masquerading as Bigby Wolf, but was met with hostile reaction by Chief Kaw-Liga's followers armed with red sticks," the would-be tv anchorman announced. "A Clintonista still embedded in the deep state controlled by the notorious Crooked Man, George Soros, accosted the Good Samaritan and charged him with…"

"We get the picture," said the judge. "Let's move on."

"Native Americans are known to be especially susceptible to the mind-altering effects of alcohol that loosen suppressed inhibitions and result in uncivilized behavior that often…"

Bang! went the judge's gavel.

"Enough 'tv news'!" he thundered.

Ohh! spectators again exclaimed.

Hmmm.

Seeing as how Andrew Jackson was no doubt looking unsympathetic to the judge, Henrietta outright suggested that he his own self might be addicted to alcohol or other mind-altering substances. In answer to the suggestion…

"True, in his essay titled *On Drunkeness*, Montaigne extols the connection between deep drinking and deep thinking — *Cum vini vis penetravit*, he wrote — but at the same time poses 'the old and pleasant question of whether the soul of a wise man can be overcome by the strength of wine?' To be on the safe side, I strictly follow Swift's endorsement of coffee 'for making us severe, grave, and philosophical.'"

Hmmm.

"What about addiction to that *Wolf Among Us Game* that you keep on playing despite outcomes you can't control?"

"Not a chance. My huge brain produces all the dopamine it can stand by simply experiencing fight-or-flight reactions to constant fear-and-anger provoked by keeping up with current events, such as…"

Uh oh.

"Democrats in Washington are again on the warpath against judges."

Ohhh…

A wad of cotton — or more likely, one of those electronic earbuds for receiving phone messages — had dropped out of

Andrew Jackson's motorcycle helmet.

"So Your Honor could be next on Senator Schumer's hit list," he said to the judge.

Ohhh!

Bang!

Henrietta collapsed into a chair and braced herself for a bad judgement.

"This Preliminary Hearing is hereby declared to be in abeyance pending evaluation of the accused's mental ability to understand the nature of his acts and the charges against him," said the judge. "During his continued confinement of at least thirty days, he shall not be allowed to consume any so-called 'news'."

Bang!

THE
END